It's About Time

A novel by

Elliott J. Anderson

Edited by Warren Anderson

Layout by Tim May

Cover art by Gabrielle Gizzi

Printed in the United States of America

ISBN-13: 978-0-915725-21-2

This novel is dedicated to my wife Angie.
A loving and committed wife and mother.
A gifted and extraordinary teacher.
An advocate for foster children.
A community meals provider.
And a wise, beautiful, and God fearing woman.

Contents

Chapter 1

Friday

Max McGovern left his high-rise condo that overlooked Lake Michigan in a rush. He was mad. He was sad. He was confused. He wasn't sure what he had packed, but he knew he had to leave for a while. He took the stairs even though he lived on the 17th floor; it was better for his cardio and fitness regimen. He gave a high five to Renaldo, the doorman and his squash partner, and revolved through the doors and out into the single-digit wind chill. Ronaldo had already called for the taxi, so Max jumped right in and headed for O'Hare. He didn't know where he was going yet, he would decide when he got to the airport, but he knew he had to get out of Chicago. It was February. It was a week from Valentine's Day. It was already bitterly cold, and a polar vortex was a couple of days away. But this trip wasn't to escape the Windy City or the wicked weather; it was to run from his broken heart and the wonderful woman who had told him three months ago that their relationship was finally over.

He shook his head sadly, sighed deeply, and slumped into the worn-out seat.

Max's boss, Frederick VanStevens, was the one who gave him the week off, and not for a joyful time of freedom, either. Fred had hired Max and knew he was a winner. Max had exceeded everyone's expectations the first couple of years and become an associate director and then a director of marketing and sales faster than anyone in the history of the 74-year-old company. But since his fiancée had broken off their engagement, Max was a shell of himself. It had been three months since Max and his team had delivered a successful pitch. The superstar was fading quickly, and this was a cutthroat business. His existing clients were not happy, and the new clients were not impressed. Fred either had to fire him or get him out of the area for a while – to heal – to find himself again. Fred told Max he would make his mind up on Max's future by how Max carried himself when he came back. He said he wanted to see the return of Max's moxie and his chutzpah. Max was grateful for a second chance but was also scared. Did he even want to do marketing and sales for big business anymore? What did it matter?

2

How was he making the world a better place? And who was he
without Abigail? And how do you have moxie and chutzpah with a
broken heart?

Abigail Richards still loved Max. She always had and she
probably always would, but the changes she saw in Max about
commitment and character were too significant to overlook. They
met in the fifth grade when Pastor Jerry, Abigail's father, had been
called to serve at Lakeside Community Church on the North Shore.
Max noticed the curly black-haired, braces-wearing beauty the very
first Sunday her family was introduced. Max's dad Mark was the
worship pastor. Both kids lived in the fishbowl of a church
community and potluck politics. They understood each other
immediately, and their friendship followed naturally and intimately.
Youth group, mission trips, and family vacations together brought
them closer, and by the time they were juniors in high school, Max
and Abigail were inseparable. It was first love. It was true love. It
was forever love. Neither of them had ever dated anyone else.

The romance blossomed and matured. They rarely argued
or fought. They were affectionate and intimate but never

inappropriate, and they never embarrassed their friends with

romance, arguments, or conflict. They always seemed to be in sync,

in rhythm, and in lockstep together. They were truly best friends.

They both attended and graduated from Northwestern, where Max

majored in marketing and Abigail in accounting. Even their majors

blended well. They dreamed of running their own marketing firm

for churches and missionaries. They even had a name and a website:

Cast the Net.

They were engaged their senior year with secret plans to be

married a year to the day of their graduation, but it never happened.

Max always had a personal or work issue that ruined the timing. The

first year, his older brother Mike got married, and Max told Abigail

that you couldn't have two McGovern weddings in the same

summer. The second year, Max had to work in Italy from April to

June, which obviously blocked the planning and details for the

second anniversary date. After those bitter disappointments, Abigail

quit planning and simply waited. After the third and fourth year, she

was really hurt, but forgave him and put it aside. And when the year-

five date approached, and Max was further away from marriage and further away from who she knew him to be, she finally had seen and observed enough. For a decade, everything had been so right, so easy, so blessed. Then, slowly, the intimacy and the unity faded. Every time Abigail brought it up, Max changed the subject or skirted the issue, until Abigail said enough time had passed and they were finished. Max was shocked, but then again, he wasn't. He was relieved. He was angry. He was exhilarated, but also devastated. He was a mess, and for the first time in his life he didn't know what he was doing with anything and everything.

Though Abigail had pulled the trigger on the break-up, she fared no better than Max with the separation. She hadn't missed a day of school, a single class, or even one day of work – for any job – ever, but after she told Max it was over, she missed several days at Anderson Accounting. She didn't think she was ever really sick, but her whole body just ached. Sometimes she could barely move, barely breathe. She often went home to see her mom, who always encouraged her with cookies and hot chocolate, but even that didn't work. She cried until there were no more tears, but she knew she had made the right decision, at least for now.

Late January and early February was also the start of the serious tax season for accountants. Her boss, Mary Anne Anderson, the founder and owner of Anderson Accounting, was not a bit pleased by this unexplained illness that took her most valuable junior accountant away from the office, and she didn't give a hill of beans about a broken heart. Mary Anne had told Abigail on more than one occasion that Max had commitment issues and was obviously not serious about making Abigail his bride, especially when the engagement wavered into the four-year plan. As far as Mary Anne was concerned, Abigail better find herself, find a new boyfriend, and find her normal commitment and work ethic fast, or she would need to find a new job.

Of course, their parents had talked all about this tragedy. They were grieving also. Everyone had assumed for the last decade that this couple was not only headed to the altar but also headed to great things together as a married couple. The parents had talked, eaten, and cried together over this change of heart, but they gave their children space to grieve, grow, and figure it out for themselves. They weren't kids anymore. They were 27. They had good jobs.

Chapter 1

They had nice cars. They had great apartments. Even though they were surprised, Jerry and Joan trusted their oldest daughter when she said her engagement to Max needed to be over. Abigail always made wise decisions, was always first-born responsible, and always thought things through because that's what accountants do and that's how left-brain thinkers make decisions. They organize data and information and put the right numbers and equations together to find the right answers and solutions. So why were they second-guessing Abigail this time? And why did something not add up?

Mark and Maisy McGovern were sad for Max also, and even though their middle son had always been a little more of a challenge than his siblings, he rarely acted ignorantly or rash. How could he let Abigail slip away? She was perfect for him. They had loved Abigail like the daughter they never had for the past 12 years. It was hard to lose her. They blamed Max but tried not to pass guilt or shame his way during this time of loss and regret. It was Max, after all, who had delayed the wedding dates, before they both agreed just to remain engaged without an eventual marriage date. Both their parents had told them that an engagement without a date wasn't really an engagement, but it was their relationship, and they had to take ownership of it. Max was creative, instinctual, and impulsive, which is why he was such a good marketer and salesman, but also why he could be hard to pin down on his convictions. It was why he was so charming and disarming but also why he could be manipulative and sneaky. It was why Abigail was such a perfect partner for him because she was the exact opposite. She was direct. She was timely and accurate. And she was always accountable to reason and order. Over the past several years, the call of the material world had started to infiltrate Max's life: the Mercedes, the lake condo, the fancy suits. They fit the job and the clients Max wooed, but none of the family thought it really fit Max. They were proud of his accomplishments but were not sure this lifestyle was best for him.

Stephanie Carter was Abigail's best friend and roommate. They had started at Anderson Accounting together five years earlier, and both of them had done very well under the tutelage of their strict and difficult boss. Stephanie didn't know the Max and Abigail of their high school or college years, but she knew the couple for the past five years and she believed in them. She could see the connection and commitment even when Max wavered, and she always supported the two of them. Stephanie was concerned, however, about the obvious burden the break-up had caused Abigail. She had hoped the shock of the separation would help Max evaluate his life choices, responding accordingly with a recommitment to win back his love. As the separation moved into four months, she was beginning to have her doubts. Stephanie tried to reassure Abigail but also encouraged her to make a profile on a dating site. This confused Abigail and even made her a little mad, but not at Stephanie; it just made her more frustrated with Max. She didn't want to start all over with someone. She had been secure in her romantic relationship and choice of a husband for a decade. What in the world had happened?

Chapter 2

Max arrived at O'Hare around 4:30 p.m., a disastrous time to travel in Chicago, which made the 15-mile drive a 45-minute experience. The delay gave Max ample time to ponder where he wanted to go, where he needed to be. He tried not to think about Abigail again, but she had been on his heart and mind for almost 15 years. How was he supposed to alter his brain waves to move her out of his daily rhythm? It was affecting his work. It was affecting every single aspect of his life. Why did it hurt so much now when for a couple of months prior to Abigail's calling it off, he had wondered what it would be like to date someone else? Now, he didn't want to even look at another woman. All he could think about was the one he had lost. What an idiot he was. Abigail was smart, kind, beautiful, talented, hard-working, family-oriented, sweet, faithful, responsible, and fun, and she loved the Lord and wanted to serve Him and her community. Would he find any woman even remotely as well-rounded and perfectly suited for him as she?

Because he wanted to go somewhere warm and familiar, Max decided to go to Cocoa Beach, Florida. It was tropical and he could rest and relax by the ocean. Besides, his uncle and aunt lived there and ran a rescue mission, so Max could help for the week and not spend too much money. He hated to sit still and just vegetate. That didn't relax him. It actually made him restless and agitated. He was a man of action and productivity. His aunt and uncle had a large, old villa-styled home they had restored right along the Atlantic coast line. Max and his family went to Cocoa Beach at least once every other year to work at the Heart and Soul Rescue Mission, right in the center of the beach community, and right next door to their house. Max needed family right now, even though he didn't want to hear how stupid and immature he had been, and his Uncle Ray always told him the truth. He found a flight leaving at 7:00 p.m., booked the ticket, and, after he had cleared security and the baggage check, texted his uncle that he was on his way. His uncle responded with only three words, but they rocked Max's world for the entirety of the flight: "It's about time."

Chapter 2

Abigail talked to Stephanie and her sisters all the time, but she didn't know where to turn or whom to talk to about her decision when it came to non-sisterly conversation. She hadn't talked to Max in three weeks now, the longest silence between them since they were 10 years old. It felt like she had lost an arm or a leg. She loved having a dad as a pastor and a mother as a social worker, but at times that made advice so plentiful and regular, it overwhelmed her need for linear processing. She had often depended on them too much for direction and guidance, and she thought at 27 she should walk through this massive marital decision on her own. On one side of her brain, she knew that was silly. She had a great family and should take advantage of that blessing. On the other side of her brain, she knew no one could make this decision for her – or even with her – so she chose not to talk to her parents about it anymore. She had watched her parents' marriage closely and knew it was worthy of its almost 40-year anniversary. The same was true with Max's parents. They argued more, and were more emotional, just like Max, but they were also headed for a forever marriage. Abigail was determined to have the same thing, a forever marriage. And if Max wasn't able to step up to that level of commitment then Max was not going to be her husband. It was super painful to recognize this truth, but she knew she had to, and Max needed to face this loss, as well. She was really struggling with the emotional pain, but her mental and rational side knew this was right. She did, however, want to talk it through with someone who loved her, knew her well, and would not judge her.

Abigail also wanted to talk with someone who knew Max well, but one who would be impartial and fair. That didn't leave many options. She wrote down a list of potential mentors to help her through this ordeal, and the obvious choice leapt off the page. Abigail decided to call Sally McGovern, Ray's wife – Max's aunt. Because the McGovern and Richards families vacationed together for years, which included frequent trips to Cocoa Beach and the mission, Abigail had formed a very close mentoring relationship with Sally McGovern. She had kept in touch with her at least monthly for almost a decade, and Abigail knew she needed to reach out to Sally for guidance and prayer. So, about 5:30 p.m., on the same Friday night that Max had texted Uncle Ray on his way to

Florida, Abigail called Sally. Even separately, Max and Abigail processed in similar ways and with similar people, and the counterbalance of the two couples was in play. Ray was an accountant and, like Abigail, more sequential and structured in thought and action. Sally was a social worker and, like Max, more relational and random in her movements. That was part of the connection with Sally for Abigail. She knew both Max and her in a variety of capacities.

The two ladies caught up quickly and easily, and Sally did not waste much time arriving at the primary issue. Like her husband, she was a straight shooter. She wanted to know why the engagement was called off and why Abigail was doubting her decision that they had talked through in confirmation just a few months earlier. They talked for over an hour – long enough that the text Max sent Ray arrived during the ladies' phone call. Ray grinned and showed Sally the text while their phone call was in progress, so it was an easy and seamless transition for Sally to invite Abigail down to Florida for some much-needed rest and relaxation. Ray left the room so his joyful laughter would not be overheard. Abigail said it sounded wonderful, but she would have to clear it with her boss and call back soon. She also didn't want Sally to tell Max she was heading down to see them. Sally assured her of that and said she hadn't talked to Max in quite a while. Thankfully, Abigail didn't ask if Ray had talked to Max.

After Abigail got off the phone and walked around the apartment straightening up the already very straightened-up living room and kitchen, she decided she really wanted to go to Florida and see Sally. The more she thought about getting away from Chicago, the winter, and her work for a while, the more excited she became. She called Stephanie to talk through the possibility, and Stephanie gave her the final push and encouragement she needed to call Mary Anne with the request – immediately, while her heart and mind were committed to the trip. Stephanie knew Abigail would change her mind if she waited until Monday. Abigail's sense of duty, order, and responsibility were so high she would talk herself out of her personal need for the needs of the company. She always did. Stephanie was just as committed to the company, but a little more balanced in her approach.

Chapter 2

Abigail was surprised, but Mary Anne was actually very supportive of the vacation, even acted as if the idea had been hers by the time they agreed on the timing and duration of the trip. She did ask Abigail to promise that when she came back, she would bring her A-game back with her. The B-game that Abigail had displayed recently was not up to Anderson's or Abigail's standard. Abigail agreed and cried a little bit, trying to hide the tears from Mary Anne, between dabs of her Kleenex thanking her profusely and assuring her she would be back to usual form when she returned. Abigail quickly called Stephanie back to tell her the great news, and the more she talked with her the giddier and sillier she became – wow, she really did need a break – and then called again with the final confirmation of the visit. Sally was super excited and celebrated with her. Ray then grabbed the cell and let Abigail know that Sally would pick her up from the Orlando International Airport at noon on Monday if she could get a ticket on United #731. Sally took the cell back and the two girls giggled about how quickly Ray had Googled the flight times and prices, determining when it was best in their schedule to pick up Abigail.

17

Max and Abigail were both heading down to Cocoa Beach, neither one knowing the other had reached out to Ray and Sally within 20 minutes of each other. Three weeks without talking to each other, but their hearts were still unified enough to recognize a similar need for holistic family love and care from dear relatives. Maybe they were still joined at the hip? Maybe this twist of fate wasn't an accident or just an amazing coincidence!

Ray and Sally held a quick conference call on Zoom with both Max's and Abigail's parents to inform the family of the ironically planned road trips. They hadn't promised Max or Abigail they wouldn't talk to the rest of the family, and they wanted the parents to know, to be excited, and to be in prayer about this divine coincidence. They all were hopeful this was just what the couple needed to find themselves and each other again. They also all agreed to fly down to join Ray and Sally and Max and Abigail at the end of the following week, just in time for Valentine's Day on Sunday because every Valentine's Day, the Heart and Soul Rescue Mission hosted a "Heart and Soul Celebration." It was a community event that gave love and compassion to the people of Cocoa Beach, but also the tourists and anyone else, for that matter, who wanted to join them. Doctors, lawyers, barbers, accountants and many other professionals donated their services for the afternoon, and the evening featured a banquet, which included a silent auction that raised money for the mission. Finally, the evening's capstone event was a "Sweet Heart" dance that always lasted well past midnight.

What Ray and Sally didn't tell them was this trip had much more at stake for them than just the relationship with Max and Abigail. The Heart and Soul Rescue Mission had been a faithful staple of hope and healing in the Cocoa community for over 30 years, but Ray and Sally were not getting any younger, and raising new support for an established mission was difficult. Over the past several years, they had lost many donors to death, retirement, or relocation, and new donors were not easily secured. There were too many needs at the Heart and Soul for Ray to travel the country looking for new donors, and he had tapped out all the local and regional investors he knew. Moreover, Ray and Sally were getting tired. They both felt it was time for new leadership to take over the mission before it was too late. Ray and Sally needed help fast, or the rescue mission was going to have to shut its doors. They both agreed they would tell Max and Abigail about that reality before the end of the week, but neither had the heart to tell them before they arrived.

Chapter 3

Max heard the familiar "ding," adjusted his seat back, turned off his air vent, and stared out the window of the 747 as the skyscrapers and lake shore disappeared. Just like his career, he thought. He tried to sleep. He tried to play games on his phone. But nothing worked. He couldn't stop thinking about Abigail, about what Uncle Ray had said, and about who he had become. Then he heard what he thought was a familiar voice as the stewardess made her way down the aisle and near his row, 37. He always liked the back of the plane – more privacy, near the bathroom – where he could watch other people, but they might not be able to watch him. Suddenly, the face that matched the voice was right in front of him. It was Martha Kingsbury, Stewardess Martha Kingsbury of United Airlines and a Lake Shore High School graduate of 2009, just like Abigail and Max. Martha was the only girl Max had ever had a crush on besides Abigail, and now she leaned over his seat flirtatiously with an ear-to-ear smile and asked the handsome man what he wanted to drink.

Martha had recognized Max immediately when he first boarded. His general look hadn't changed since 10th grade, so it was not a difficult task. Max asked for water, and they chit-chatted while Martha served the rest of the row. As she prepared to move down the aisle, Martha told Max she was on a layover in Orlando that night, so she could have a drink with him when they landed. It was more a relational order than a social suggestion, so Max felt obligated to say yes, even though he really wasn't in the mood. Martha was almost always bubbly and happy, and it had been at least 10 years since they had talked about anything significant. Furthermore, Max didn't want to be happy or cheery right now, and right before Max started to date Abigail, he had asked Martha to a homecoming dance. Martha had said no, but Max always felt weird about that because a few weeks later, he asked Abigail and for the rest of high school he and Abigail were an item. That one vulnerable experience had made Max a little awkward around Martha at reunions and when they ran into each other at church or in the community. And even though they didn't see each other very often and had never dated, they still had great communication chemistry and natural attraction to each other. All the more reason, Max thought, he should have said no to the meeting, but then again Martha always found a way to get what she wanted, so he probably saved himself 10 minutes of a debate by simply saying yes to the initial offer. With that reconciled analysis, Max finished his snack and leaned back for a nap.

Regretfully, at least in Martha's eyes, she had already said yes to the quarterback of Lake Shore High, Joe Baker, one lousy day before Max had asked her to homecoming, so she had to watch two of her friends become the homecoming king and queen and the Lake Shore Couple of the Decade. Martha wasn't jealous, but she was envious, and she had also seen on Instagram some posts from classmates that said the king and queen of Lake Shore had royally called it quits. Martha was not a predator, but she was also 27 and eager to find a good man to marry, and Max fit the bill in about every category possible. Throughout the rest of her shift she planned her strategy for quick relational intimacy but recognized that Max was probably grieving, so she would need to be sensitive to his emotions.

After his nap, Max felt better and pondered the relational connection in front of him. Max had forgotten that Martha was a stewardess, and specifically one with United, but he hadn't forgotten her good looks or her smile. The more he thought about it, the more he wondered if this was what he needed – a talkative friend and a beautiful woman to take his mind off Abigail. And what were the odds that Martha would be working this random flight on a Friday night? Maybe this was a providential occurrence? He began to get a little excited to spend some time with her but also pretty nervous. He had never been on an official date with anybody other than Abigail. But this wasn't a date, was it? Martha made eye contact with Max every time she had the chance and smiled more fully and more flirtatiously every time. Uh oh, Max thought, this was a date.

Abigail felt great peace and comfort knowing she was headed to Cocoa Beach to see Sally, who had always been such a wise and calming influence on her. Abigail smiled for the first time that day and then called her mom to tell her the big surprise. Joan's response was subdued and mild, not completely foreign to her counselor spirit, but pretty restrained considering this spontaneous move from her non-spontaneous oldest daughter. Abigail was a little startled that her mother didn't question the decision more, but she was too excited about the trip to care. After 10 minutes of gentle and persistent imploring, Abigail finally relented and agreed to the invitation to pop over and eat some chocolate chip cookies with her little sister Phoebe. Joan had used Phoebe as a pawn to connect with her over-achieving, over-committed, and over-responsible Abigail for years. It was hard for Abigail not to be there for Phoebe in her high school years – and now, her senior year, in particular. Once Abigail heard and saw Phoebe in the background of her mother's FaceTime call – begging her to come over, elbow deep in flour – she knew she had to drive the five miles up the shore to visit. But why didn't her mother act more surprised when Abigail told her she was flying to Florida on Monday, especially, since she was visiting Max's aunt and uncle?

Ray and Sally hadn't been this excited in weeks. It had been a really tough start to the new year. Their business administrator, Brad Bixby, had left work the last Friday in January and hadn't been heard from since. They found out soon thereafter that $10,000 dollars was missing from their ever-dwindling savings account, but Brad hadn't returned any of their calls, texts, or e-mails. It was so unlike him. The amount of money stolen didn't concern them that much, though it was a lot of money for the struggling rescue mission. It was the dishonesty, fraudulent behavior, and deceitful relationship that bothered Ray and Sally the most. They prayed about the situation for a day before deciding not to file a police report. If Brad needed the money for something crucial, then they would release that money to him and the Lord and let the matter go. It wasn't easy to do at this time in their ministry and at this time of the year. They weren't anywhere near ready for the Heart and Soul Celebration, and Brad had done a great job with that event the last few years. Now, they were short money and short personnel for the major fundraising event of the year. And probably for the same reason Brad stole or misappropriated the money, he had been way behind on the planning and commitments for the Valentine's Day event when he left. Losing Brad was like losing a son for Ray and Sally. They were still grieving him and wondered where he was and what had happened. Ray had crafted an e-mail to the city council announcing the elimination of the event but hadn't sent it yet. They were waiting over the weekend to make the final call, but as soon as

Ray received the text from Max, he deleted the letter. After Sally finished the final arrangements with Abigail, Sally and Ray grabbed their glasses of wine and headed out to the veranda, happier than they had been in months. Help was on the way. Max and Abigail were headed to them for selfish reasons, but the reality was they were going to be a huge help to the mission. They had prayed for the Lord to intervene and He had. Now, they prayed the Lord would save the marriage of their nephew and his former fiancée.

On the way over to her mother's house, Abigail wondered why she was so excited to help with the Heart and Soul Valentine's Day Celebration. She had jumped at the chance to help Sally pull off the event when Sally mentioned it toward the end of their phone call. Sally and Abigail agreed the celebration would be the perfect distraction and stress release for her. Besides, Abigail reminded Sally, she had fun memories of participating in the Heart and Soul Celebration twice before – the last one when she and Max were sophomores in college. It was at that sweetheart dance when Max had first pitched "the year after graduation anniversary" wedding idea. Tears rolled down Abigail's cheeks as she pulled into the driveway, still reminiscing. She wiped away the tears and the memories, took a deep breath, and saw the door open as she wandered up the walkway. It was always good to come home for a while.

Max waited in the bookstore for Martha to finish up her stewardess duties. Always an avid reader before, Max hadn't picked up a book in a year. He looked over a few mysteries with interesting titles but didn't feel any compulsion to read them, so he tossed them back on the table and wandered aimlessly around the store. A few minutes later, Martha strutted into the store with a form-fitting aqua-colored dress and a confident and determined look. She gave Max a huge and aggressive hug that lasted longer than he wanted it to and then interlocked their arms and dragged him across the current of weary travelers and safely into the airport lounge. Max started to feel sick to his stomach. He had a gut feeling that this was not a wise move, but he lacked the conviction and confidence to do anything about it. While he followed Martha through the crowded lounge, he texted his uncle that he had arrived safely, was catching up with a friend, and would be there in an hour or so and not to wait up for

him.

Chapter 4

Saturday

By the time Max woke up Saturday morning, Ray and Sally were already at the rescue mission and busy in their normal routines. Sally had left Max a plate of food, re-heating instructions, a cup of coffee, and a Heart and Soul Rescue Mission polo shirt. It was 10:00 a.m. Max ate quickly, slipped on the shirt, and headed out the screen door and across the patio to the mission. He had avoided anything stupid the night before, but he wasn't completely sure what he had told Martha about Abigail, the mission, or his intentions. It was totally unfamiliar territory for him to mingle with a different woman other than Abigail. It had him very nervous, but he didn't have to worry about that anymore. He probably wouldn't ever see Martha again, although they had updated their contact information and Martha had assured him she would get a hold of him again soon. He shook his head, though no one was looking, and put Martha and her gorgeous smile out of his mind for the time being. He was really glad to be in Florida, away from work, helping his aunt and uncle, who had always been two of his favorite people. He felt a joy in his heart. He felt a skip to his step. It was something he hadn't felt in Chicago for quite a while, and it wasn't just because it was already 65 degrees.

Saturdays at the Heart and Soul Rescue Mission were for the kids. There were several tutors available. There were craft rooms. There was a game room. There was a library and computer lounge. Max's company had provided the computer lounge shortly after Max had started his job there and he had told Fred about the mission. And the indoor and outdoor basketball courts were packed with teen-age boys. Max had brought basketball to the rescue mission and convinced his uncle to invest in the outdoor hoops, along with the already existing indoor ones left over from the YMCA, which used to own the mission's property. Max had been a good high school basketball player and still played in a men's league with his friends, so he gravitated to the outdoor courts. His timing was impeccable, as he immediately had to separate a couple of strong-headed and strong-bodied young men in a heated, testosterone-fueled argument. Max saw the need and headed over to the supply closet, grabbed a referee shirt and a whistle, and officiated games for the next two hours. He was hot, he was sweaty, and the kids whined and complained about every call he made, but Max was having a blast.

Abigail had a hard time Saturday morning. She had slept well and did her normal morning yoga and walk time with Stephanie, but she then had no heart or energy to do any of the accounting work she had brought home – something, unfortunately, she had to do almost every weekend. She had wanted to leave right away, but Sally had told her to come on Monday and was firm with the time. While Abigail made her morning smoothie, she suddenly had a great idea. Would her sister Missy want to go also? She was a fantastic event planner and public relations whiz who had graduated from the University of Chicago two years ago and already owned her own company. Missy was organized and detailed, just like Abigail, and she also had been burned by a previous boyfriend and poured herself into her work. She needed to get away and didn't have to check with a boss, so Sally thought she had a good chance to talk Missy into joining her in Florida. Without even asking Sally first, Abigail showered, got dressed, and drove down to Missy's condo on

Michigan Avenue and did, indeed, proceed to persuade her sister to join her on the beach. By the end of the night, the two girls had been on a couple of conference calls with Sally and had the whole week laid out and ready for action. Abigail hadn't felt this happy since Christmas, and Missy was so excited she demanded to spend the night with her older sister. Abigail happily obliged and the girls drove back up the Lake Shore with Missy's suitcases already in Abigail's car.

Max had showered and was eating lunch on the veranda when Ray finally had time to come over and join him. He thanked Max for supervising the basketball games and asked him if he could spend some time in the computer lab in the afternoon. Some kids were creating the publicity and marketing posters for the Valentine's Day Celebration, and even though everything was late, Ray really wanted the kids to have the chance to have their work shown in the beach store windows and hoped that some late publicity for the event was better than no publicity at all. Max was glad to help out and told Ray there were some excellent players on the courts. He asked Ray if the mission still sponsored the Cocoa Beach

Community Basketball League. Ray sadly told him they had to cancel the league last year. They didn't have the funding or the coaches to run the program anymore. That news really bothered Max, and he told Ray if he lived down there, he would take it over for him and fund it himself. Both men smiled at the thought, and Max wondered out loud why Ray had not called him and asked him for a donation for the program last year. Ray said because even if he had the money to run the program, he didn't have the coaches.

After some silence, while standing in the ocean breeze, Max asked Ray what he had meant by his text to him last night, "It's about time." Ray shook his head slowly, sipped on his tea, smiled and told Max that he would know – when he knew. He then laughed and left Max alone on the veranda while he went in the kitchen to get a sandwich. Max sat isolated and alone for a while, enjoying the sun and the breeze. He checked his phone for the temperature in Chicago. It was 7 degrees there and 77 in Cocoa. He had made the right decision. He checked his email and answered a few non-urgent requests and then headed over to the computer room. Max stayed with the students until about 3:00 p.m., and though he didn't have great tech skills, he definitely knew what communication worked for marketing and what didn't. He was impressed with the students' abilities in graphics and sign-making. They had created some pretty cool posters and were very proud of their work. He helped them with slight changes here and there, but, overall, left them alone to give them complete ownership of their work.

Max went back to his room after helping the kids and spent the late afternoon by himself. He read his Bible for the first time that year and earnestly prayed to God for direction and peace amidst his turmoil. He then decided to walk alone along the beach. He strolled through the business district. For the first time in a long time, he was doing some soul searching, and he wasn't super excited about what the search found. He admitted he was lonely. He recognized he was really sad. He seethed with frustration, mostly at himself, and did some deep breathing while he walked to calm his spirit. He had a great job, but he didn't love working there, and often he was bored with the goals of profit margin and successful pitches. The car, condo, racquet club membership, and all the other perks were great, but they didn't make him happy, didn't fulfill him;

yet they had slowly, unintentionally become an integral part of his life, and that was scary. It all happened accidentally because he had not been vigilant to guard his heart from the lure of power, money, and material possessions that had slowly taken over his life, and it made Max sick. He knew his parents were proud of him, but probably disappointed. He knew his brothers loved him, but they were distant of late. Most importantly, he knew he had broken Abigail's heart on multiple occasions. He had to make some changes soon – for work, for Abigail, but mainly for himself. The sun had disappeared over the ocean and he finally checked his phone. He was shocked. No wonder he was hungry. It was after 9 pm! He had been searching his soul for over five hours.

When he returned to Ray and Sally's they were waiting up for him, watching the news. Sally had fresh brownies laid out and Ray immediately went to get the Butter Pecan ice cream out of the freezer. It felt like high school again, when his aunt and uncle would bribe Max and his brothers with sweet treats, so they'd have time to communicate, challenge, and encourage their nephews. Max accepted the treats and slumped in the couch across from Sally.

When he finished the dessert, he reversed the normal meal order and asked her to make him a sandwich. Sally apologized for the backwards meal, but both laughed at the late night, teenage-boy-styled dinner.

Even though it was late, Ray started to challenge Max about his life and direction before he even swallowed the first bite of his triple-decker BLT. Ray asked why Max's life was a mess right now and why in the world he hadn't married Abigail? And he didn't wait for Max to answer, summarizing in two minutes what Max had just pondered over the last five hours. It was as if Ray looked right into his soul, and it was probably the reason why Max had felt led to come to Florida in the first place. He needed the accountability. He needed the mentor. He needed the conviction. Max stared at Ray for a long time while chewing his food and without saying a word. He was frozen in his thoughts and not sure where to start. Ray interjected again and, with great intensity, passionately laid out three of the main areas of mess in Max's life.

"First, you haven't married Abigail. Now she's broken it off with you, and you realize you probably have let the best thing in your life walk away – and only your selfish pride caused the

separation. Second," Ray continued, "you obviously are bored and

tired of big business and realize that all of the money and all of the

possessions don't satisfy the soul." Max was already drilled right

between the eyes, but Ray wasn't finished. "Third, your trust and

faith in the Lord is waning, your commitment to church and

community is weak, and you've lost your passion for loving and

serving others." And with that, Ray hugged him and said he was

going to bed.

It really hurt, but "This is why I came to Florida," Max

thought. It wasn't about the fun and the sun, though that would be

great also, he was sure. It was about tough but truthful, loving but

challenging conversations with his aunt and uncle. If his parents had

talked to him that way, Max would have interrupted them, defended

himself, argued and yelled, and eventually stormed out of the room.

But with an aunt and uncle, there is a softer boundary line, an easier

path to listening and receiving. Max loved and trusted his parents,

but he needed Ray and Sally's advice and wisdom this time, and they

were giving it to him in spades. Max talked to Sally until after midnight and felt heard, understood, and appreciated. He also felt inspired and motivated to slowly pursue Abigail again, though Sally had never specifically coached him to do that. He would think about calling or texting soon, but, in the meantime, he was going to pour himself into the Valentine's Celebration week of preparation.

Stephanie joined Missy and Abigail Saturday night, and they laid out the ten cutest outfits Abigail owned and displayed them across the kitchen table, telling her to pick the best seven for the trip. They also grabbed two of her best formal dresses. One was a stately green and the other a romantic red. Abigail said she didn't need her best clothes down there, as she folded up her jeans and sweatshirts, but her sister and best friend would not be denied. Abigail didn't plan on going on any dates. She was headed to Florida to work in a mission and in the community. The more she thought about it, though, the sadder Abigail became. The idea of a date with anyone other than Max hadn't been on her mind for over a decade.

Chapter 5

Sunday

Sunday morning arrived early. That's what happens when three friends talk until two in the morning. Abigail told Stephanie and Missy she was ready to go to Lakeside Community Church for the first time since the break-up. Stephanie asked if she could tag along, and after calling Phoebe, the three daughters of the senior pastor who gave the message that morning sat with their parents in the staff row for the first time in many years. Phoebe was so happy to have her big sisters there with her. Mike and Matt McGovern, the older and younger brothers of Max, were also at the service with their parents. Usually when they were there, the boys played special music. Only Max, of the "Lakeshore Brady Bunch," as they used to call themselves, was missing. The three McGovern men who were present played a moving version of "Amazing Grace" during the service. Abigail had forgotten how musically talented and gifted the McGoverns were. After the service, Abigail said hello to Mark and Maisy with big hugs and a few tears, but they kept the conversation

41

about everything else other than Max. And just like old times, both families went to Portillo's together after the service, laughing and telling stories about each other and their adventures together while enjoying traditional Chicago hot dogs. It was a great Sunday. It reminded her of the old days, and she wondered why they didn't still hang out together. Was a busy life really worth the absence of the family and friendship? Stephanie fit right in like a part of the family and didn't find Matt unattractive, either. She had often gone with Abigail to church, but not to Lakeside.

The service at the mission was less polished, less attended, and less structured, but for Max, he heard just what he needed to from Pastor Ray. The message happened to be about making decisions in a time of challenge or crisis. After the service, Max, Ray, and Sally walked along the beach and talked about Abigail and how Max had processed life since the confrontation and challenge the night before. Max shared with them many challenges and questions he had stewed over in his head for years. It felt so freeing and beneficial to share and process with his aunt and uncle. They were never judgmental, but they had a way of getting to the heart of any matter and made you really think about your life, while holding very

strongly and clearly to Biblical principles of love and relationships.

After a half hour or so they meandered back to the veranda, changed

clothes, and headed over to the mission to feed well over 200 people

for the Sunday community meal – another tradition at the mission

that Ray said was in jeopardy of being eliminated. The meal wasn't

super expensive, but it was time consuming, and the main

underwriters of the meal had dropped away years ago. Max put on

his apron and served meals for a couple of hours. He then helped

wash the dishes, mopped the floor, and he even sat and talked with

a few of the older men who had stuck around to play checkers –

something he loved to do when he was a teenager when he visited

the mission with his family.

Reginald and Felipe had been coming to the Sunday

afternoon meal for a couple of decades and always finished the

afternoon off with some games of chess or checkers. Reginald and

Felipe, both widowers, had become best friends while serving the

country together in the Vietnam War. While enduring those awful

experiences and hardships, they had vowed to make it back to

Florida to start their own construction company, and that's exactly what they did. Their wives and children had also grown up together, and two of their sons now ran the company. That's why the two men had taken such a liking to the McGoverns and Richardses when they visited. They reminded Reginald and Felipe of the Johnson and Lopez clans. Though it had been at least seven years since they had seen him, both men recognized Max as soon as he walked in the door and called him over for a couple of hugs, laughs, and pointed questions. Max told them he had to serve but would join them when he was finished with his chores. They laughed and told him where they would be all afternoon, looking over their shoulders toward the game tables.

Neither of the men liked to talk about the war, but other than that, no topic was off limits. They offered amazing life wisdom and always seemed to be restful, peaceful, and at home with each other and anybody else who ever wanted to talk. They wanted to hear about Abigail, of course, and were distraught and discouraged by the news their relationship had ended. Reginald reiterated that he could not believe it was true, and he said he would not accept it.

44

He had always thought he would receive an invitation to the wedding, and he and Felipe had committed to the wedding trip to Chicago whenever it was time. Why, Max thought, was he able to tell these old timers exactly what was going on in his life when he had hidden it from most of his colleagues at work for at least two months? Why did these men, who came to the mission for a free meal because of very fragile finances and a shallow bank account, have more peace and contentment than Max, who was making more money in a week than these two did in a year? What did he really want to do with his life? Who did he want to be? And whom did he want to love? What was his passion and purpose? He realized he had lost the answers to all these questions, and he had no one to blame but himself. As he sat quietly and deep in reflection, watching Reginald and Felipe exchange kings, a beautiful red-headed woman plopped down in the seat beside him. It was Martha.

Max was dumbfounded and just stared at Martha for a minute, as did Reginald and Felipe. It was hard not to stare at her. Finally, Max introduced Martha while Reginald and Felipe straightened up the table. Max wondered how Martha had found him until she reminded him he had told her the name of the mission. Martha's flights to New York had been canceled due to the severe weather, so she cashed in a week of vacation, looked up the mission, and drove on over to find him. Max was taken aback by both her beauty and her assertive nature; but right now, he wasn't sure he wanted her to be a part of this experience. Reginald and Felipe, however, were thrilled to have this intruder – they couldn't keep their eyes off her – and as the resident flirters of the rescue mission, they fussed over Martha as if she were a visiting princess. Martha was not the least bit offended by their attention; in fact, she adored it and flirted right back. Although Max had enjoyed his time with her at the airport lounge, and always loved time with Reginald and Felipe, he thought this scene was not how it was supposed to be. It should be Abigail sitting with them. He was glad he felt this way but was also confused by it. His spontaneous connecting with Martha at the airport was supposed to be an aberration, not the start of any kind of relationship, but that didn't seem to fit the intention for Martha, if he was reading her eye contact and body language accurately.

Chapter 5 - Sunday

Max finally dragged Martha away from her new admirers and took her over to meet Ray and Sally. Of course, Ray and Sally were extremely gracious and hospitable, and once Sally knew Martha was available for the week, she invited Martha to stay for dinner, then for the night, and then for the whole week. Besides, Sally said, they needed a lot of help for the Valentine's Day Celebration and proceeded to tell Martha all about the event. Martha loved community events and gobbled up every single morsel of the meal and the history of the Valentine's Day Celebration Sally delivered. Ray looked at Max, caught his attention, and then looked at Martha and gave Max a sly smile. Max tried not to smile or laugh, but he totally understood what Ray was inferring. No wonder Max stayed a while at the airport after his flight arrived in Orlando, Ray thought. They agreed together that Martha would stay for the week – in the guest room – right next to Max's room. Sometimes Max wished his aunt and uncle weren't so wonderfully hospitable to everybody.

Abigail, Stephanie, Missy, and Phoebe had a sleep over on Sunday night, this time at Phoebe's house. And now, all three daughters were headed to Florida to help put the Valentine's Day

Celebration together. Stephanie wanted to go but knew there was no way Mary Anne would give her the week off also. Jerry and Joan thought it was a worthwhile experience to let Phoebe join her sisters at the mission and miss a week of high school. Sally and Ray were overjoyed with the generosity of the Richards girls. They were all high-energy, get-things-done ladies, and there was no doubt anymore whether they would to be able to have a great Valentine's Day Celebration. In just two days, Ray and Sally had recruited, mostly incidentally, Max, Abigail, Martha, Missy, and Phoebe, five high-powered, Type-A, driven, professional, hard-working, gifted friends and family members. Jerry and Joan agreed to drive their daughters to the airport and told them they would join them at the end of the week. No need for that surprise to be a secret any longer. It explained to Abigail why her mother had not been more surprised by her decision to fly south. But still, none of the girls knew what Jerry and Joan did, but failed to mention, that Max was already at the mission! And none of the Chicagoans, except Max, knew Martha Kingsbury was there also! There were a lot of surprises in store for everyone.

Max, Martha, Ray, and Sally talked for a long time on Sunday night. It wasn't like two couples talking; it was more like Ray and Sally getting to know Martha in their Ray-and-Sally manner. That meant that Martha was pretty much going to lay her whole life story out before them whether she intended to or not. Max didn't do much talking, but he did learn a ton about Martha that he had never known before. He took note of the techniques Ray and Sally used for their disclosure-inducing mentoring. They asked simple questions of genuine interest and then found themes and patterns and gently pointed them out or reflected on stories Martha shared that must have been difficult. For example, Martha's mom and dad had died in a bad car accident when she was in college. Max had no idea about that loss and felt terrible he had not been able to offer his sympathy. Following that tragedy, Martha had stopped pursuing her interior design degree at University of Illinois and moved back home to help her brother and sister finish high school at Lakeshore. She worked at a coffee shop, using her earnings along with the life insurance money to provide for her brother and sister and help them get into their colleges of choice. After that successful mothering duty, she wanted to do something free and exotic, so she became a stewardess. That also explained why she wasn't married. She vowed not to get involved with a man until after her siblings were out of college. She also vowed to marry a man of adventure. Both of her siblings had graduated within the past two years, and she fully admitted that she was on the hunt for a husband. With her looks and her positivity, Sally told her finding one wasn't going to be a problem. Finding the right one, however, would be harder. Finding a man who could lead her, love her, comfort her, challenge her, and complement her would be the tougher challenge. Martha soaked up this mothering every bit as much as Max did when he was the focus of Sally's maternal attention. She desperately missed her own mother and knew that this time with Ray and Sally was just what she needed.

Chapter 6

Monday

Max and Ray rose early on Monday, ate a quick breakfast Sally had left for them, and went straight to the job co-op site to see if they could find some temp work for some of the men who stayed at the mission. Reginald and Felipe used to employ as many of the men as they could, especially the veterans. But since their retirement, their sons had not continued that tradition, which disappointed them. Ray and Max also hung up the celebration posters and advertisements Max and the young students had finished on Saturday. When Ray had to run back to the mission to handle an emergency, Max decided to stay in the town and see if he could find any last-minute sponsors. He walked the stores for several hours, but having been turned down a few times, he decided he needed to think outside of the box. He also wanted to visit Reginald and Felipe's sons, but he knew they wouldn't be at their office on a workday since they were certainly on a job site somewhere. Though he was disappointed he'd have to catch them another day, he noticed he had pep and energy in his step as he walked the streets, and it wasn't just the 78-degree weather, either. He felt the renewal and refreshment in his spirit and soul because his business mind was being used for something other than the bottom line. It also felt great to be in sandals and shorts, a startling contrast to Chicago in February, where the temperatures were below zero with wind chills in the negative teens. Maybe he was just getting old, but Max could understand why so many retirees left the upper Midwest and northern states and came down to Florida to finish out their days.

On his way back toward the mission right around noon, Max passed a bar and grill where a pretty good band was playing some country music. Max was hungry and loved the harmonies of the vocalists, so he ventured in to order a burger and a beer and enjoy some more time in reflection and contemplation. After the meal but before he paid his check, Max thought of a brilliant idea, at least it was to him. What if his brothers came down with their band to play for the Valentine's Day dance? Ray had not booked a DJ or a band yet, and really, at this late date before the dance, a band was likely out of the question. Finding a respectable and affordable DJ was on the massive "to do" list he had seen on Sally's desk, though he didn't know that Abigail and Missy were the master planners of that document. After a lengthy phone call, including a promise the temperature was expected to be in the 80's all week, the band agreed to drive down if Max was willing to pay for gas, food, and the gig. Max couldn't believe they agreed, but he guessed the chance to escape the winter in the Windy City with an all-expenses-paid gig to Cocoa Beach was a pretty attractive offer. Either way, Max was super happy and couldn't wait to hang out with his brothers, let alone enjoy their music. Man, when was the last time they had all played and sung together? It had to have been four or five years. Abigail would have remembered if she were there. She had been the band's accountant in the early years. Max texted Ray and Sally to let them know the band was set for the dance and that four more strong, young men would be available to help with the event by Thursday. Sally and Ray looked at each other when they read the text and laughed out loud. All of the kids were coming down to the mission at the same time, each with separate plans, none knowing the rest of the clan members were also on their way. Max suddenly had the desire to call Abigail and tell her about it, but after almost

pressing her name on the screen multiple times, he decided against

it and put his phone away.

Sally had Martha jump into the cooking for the mission

breakfast and then took her down the street to help at the women's

shelter. Martha had never been so tired, so scared, and so

invigorated before 10:00 a.m. before. Sally had a way of making you

do anything that she wanted without intimidating you, convincing

you, or pestering you. It's as if she could see right through you and

what you needed to do in order to become who you were supposed

to become. When Sally said she had to take the mission van to the

airport to pick up a family coming to visit, Martha assumed she was

supposed to go also and dutifully followed. Sally asked her if she

would drive and Martha, of course, complied. But right before they

were to leave, Sally announced she couldn't go and politely ordered

Martha to go for her. And right as she shut the van door, she

casually mentioned that the family was Abigail and her sisters while

giving Martha the sign with the mission name and logo on it, telling

her to hold it up at the baggage claim. This was a classic ploy of

Sally's, having two people who might have some tension between them forced to relate and communicate with each other under strange and uncomfortable circumstances. Sally also assumed correctly from short comments the night before that Abigail and Martha were competitive in high school since the rules of feminine-beauty comparison required it. Martha wasn't thrilled about the assignment, but an airport run was the least she could do for the free room and board for the week.

Max left the pub and walked into a park to sit on a bench and brainstorm donor-relation strategies for the event. Especially since he had just invested a couple of thousand dollars in the process, his interest and business mind wanted to see a big profit for his aunt and uncle. Max's outside-the-box thinking had led him to consider larger donors from outside the Cocoa Beach area, so he spent an hour or so writing down all the clients he had worked with over the past five years who had huge profit margins and hearts for communities in need. Max settled on one very unique company with an extremely unique CEO. This company, a highly successful eatery, and its leader would be his primary target since Max had worked with them on a highly successful campaign about two years earlier.

Big Beef Steakhouse's corporate headquarters were in Orlando, Max thought, so he Googled them and found it was only an hour past the airport. Max looked up their number, called and asked for the CEO, Jim "Big Beef" Williams, and, to his surprise, actually caught him in the office. Jim was thrilled to hear from Max, remembered him well – even asking about Abigail and absolutely letting Max have it for the break-up – and told Max to come right over. He'd give Max 10 minutes if he could get there in under two hours. Max was already jogging back to the mission when he finally was able to get off the phone. Big Beef loved to tell big stories, so you didn't hang up on Jim until he was ready to be done. Men with millions and millions of dollars and homes in four different regions of the country were used to dictating both the time and the tenor of conversations, and Max was happy to oblige. Max had no problem with these unspoken wealth-management communication rules and was actually quite adept with them. It was part of the reason he was so successful in his job. (Or at least he was until Abigail dumped him.) Max hustled back to Ray and Sally's, but they were gone. He showered fast, changed clothes into a more traditional sales look, grabbed the spare

keys to Ray's VW in the garage, and took off for Orlando. As was

his usual practice, he simply texted his uncle after he had already

made his decision and was on his way. His uncle responded quickly

and succinctly with, "It's about time," though this time the quipped

phrase was followed with smiley face, prayer hands, and strong arm

emojis. Max grinned and threw the phone to the passenger seat to

make sure he didn't drive dangerously and illegally with his phone.

He pushed the old bug as fast as she would travel, keeping within

reasonable distance of the 75-mph speed limit. Florida drivers didn't

drive like Chicagoans, and Max wasn't sure how he felt about that as

he tried to stay patient with law-abiding citizens on the tollway.

Abigail and her sisters had a great time on the flight. It was

probably a better time than the other passengers wanted them to

have, as all the girls were boisterous and laughed a lot. Regardless

of the social inconvenience to the other passengers, by the time they

arrived at Orlando International Airport, they were tired, and their

jaws hurt from giggling. They had agreed to meet Aunt Sally at the

baggage claim, so they worked their way to their pickup carousel and waited patiently with all the other travelers. In the midst of their people-watching, Missy saw a woman holding a Heart and Soul Rescue Mission sign, but it wasn't Sally. Abigail wheeled around to see who it was, and her jaw dropped – Martha Kingsbury! They went to meet her, and after some pleasantries and reintroductions, Abigail asked the obvious question: What in the world was Martha doing at the Heart and Soul mission, and how did she know their Sally? Martha quickly replied that she had run into Max on a flight down to Orlando on Friday, and he had invited her to come stay with him at Uncle Ray's and Aunt Sally's. Abigail tried to hide her reaction to that news, but she soon realized that her mouth had dropped open, her eyes had watered, and her heart might have hit the floor. Abigail was too stunned to ask any follow-up questions, but Missy and Phoebe took over from there and peppered Martha with 15 minutes of questions while they waited for their luggage. Abigail tried not to listen to the explanation, but she hung on every word, unsure of which emotion was winning the moment. Was it her excitement that Max was in Cocoa for the week also? Or was it anger and shock that Max had invited Martha to stay with him at the mission? By the time they had gathered all their designer matching luggage together, Abigail was convinced Martha was being honest about the coincidental meeting, but she was not the least bit happy regardless. This was her time to be with Sally, her time to be with family. This was not time to compete with Martha again for anything, communication, attention, admiration, or, of course, Max.

When Max arrived at the Big Beef Steakhouse headquarters, he wasn't nervous or anxious as he normally was for presentations. He didn't have any presentation to give. All he had was his heart and soul for the Heart and Soul Rescue Mission and 10 minutes with the CEO, the same man who had signed off on his marketing and branding plan, which had spiked sales over 10% in just a few months – converting into millions of dollars in new revenue. He felt free and liberated and looked forward to the opportunity. Max only stood in the immaculate and lush waiting room for about two minutes before being called into the conference room, so he didn't have time to finish reading all the awards on the wall for philanthropy and sales success. To his surprise, there were six executives in the room. Jim "Big Beef" Williams sat in the middle and pronounced that anything that Max McGovern found important enough for an emergency 10-minute meeting mandated the attention of his entire executive team for at least an hour. He had cleared out his schedule and demanded his leadership team do the same. Max had made him millions and deserved his full attention. "Besides," he said, "my gut instinct tells me Max must have some great ideas brewing for him to spontaneously call in this manner." Max – stunned and, of course, impressed – tried not to think about the enormous opportunity in front of him. Jim's instincts had created an empire worth several billion dollars, so who was going to question "Big Beef" when he had a hunch about Max and this surprise? Nobody!

By the time Max left the conference room 90 minutes later, he had secured a $10,000 gift for immediate use, a catered meal for the Valentine's banquet, a new underwriter for the Sunday community meal – Big Beef was opening a new restaurant in Cocoa Beach at the end of the year, so it was a perfect time for a local investment – and an annual sponsorship for the rescue mission of $20,000 for each of the next five years, a total gift package of

$150,000 with likely more to follow. Max was amazed at the afternoon's development. He skipped down the stairs and almost danced out of the lobby and into the parking lot. This was an even better feeling than the deals he closed for VanStevens because those profits always went to the firm. These gifts and profits were going to the people of the mission, the people who needed them the most. This was a deal that helped the people of Cocoa Beach and the Heart and Soul Rescue Mission. Max called Ray on his way to the car and shared with him the fantastic news. Ray informed him that the Big Beef Steakhouse gift was the largest gift secured for the mission in the last four years. After they hung up, Max became emotional and nearly cried, something he rarely ever did. In fact, he didn't think he had cried in several years, even when Abigail broke his heart. He gathered himself, hopped into Ray's car, and reached for his cell phone before turning the key over in the ignition. This time he didn't stop himself. He instinctively pressed Abigail's number.

Chapter 7

The luggage was piled up into the mission's van by several admiring and fawning service men who happened to be on the same flight and followed the girls out of the terminal. The four ladies were striking, their hair color representing the four primary colors of feminine beauty: Martha with her red hair, Abigail with the black curls, Phoebe with brown hair, and Missy with her blonde locks, albeit aided by an over-the-counter-induced tint for the otherwise chestnut brown roots. The ladies enjoyed the attention, and all appropriately flirted and thanked the men. Abigail joined Martha in the front seat. She was still shocked at Martha's disclosure about Max, and though Martha asked her repeatedly if she was alright, but her revelation about Max had clearly shaken Abigail. Not that Martha minded completely. She was competitive – and so was Abigail – and she wanted to get in the first move if they had to compete for Max's attention. Abigail told her the truth about her feelings, without saying too much, and told her the main issue at the moment was that she needed something to eat. Martha signaled off at the very next exit and they stopped at a Big Beef Steakhouse. Abigail told Missy what she wanted to eat so they could order without her and excused herself to go to the restroom. She was so mad and confused that she couldn't even cry. She was trying to fix her hair and put some fresh make-up on, continuously looking at herself in the mirror, when her phone rang. It was Max!

Abigail said hello but was very guarded and quiet. Max proceeded to tell her that he was down in Florida with his aunt and uncle and working for the mission for a week. He was so excited. He was so happy. She hadn't heard him like that in at least a year, and he didn't even seem phased to be talking with her. They hadn't talked in almost a month, but he hadn't bothered to mention that stretch of time or the fact that they were not a couple right now. He was talking to her as a friend, as the best friends they used to be. He told her all about the sponsorship from Big Beef Steakhouse, and though she was still appalled about the presence of Martha in this story, she couldn't help but smile at the irony of her location at the moment of this disclosure. She decided not to mention that or that she and her sisters were in Florida also. He would know soon

enough, but, wow, it was really good to talk to him again. The
conversation was fantastic – she didn't want to stop talking with him
– but Phoebe came in to tell her that her food was getting cold. They
were awkward with their good-byes, but other than that, it had been
their best conversation since before Thanksgiving. Max squeezed
an "I miss you" right before he hung up, hoping Abigail had heard
it. She had, and she smiled as she followed Phoebe back to the table.

Abigail sat down with a much more confident spirit now and though
she really wanted to tell Martha about the phone call from Max, she
decided against it.

Max grinned and sang praise songs for the hour drive back
to the mission. He also played the latest drop from his brother's
band on his phone. They were really good, but he could make them
better he thought. As he approached the exit for the mission,
another idea hit him without context or justification, and he knew
he had to pursue it. Instead of heading south on I-95 to Cocoa
Beach, Max went north instead toward Daytona Beach. Since it was
close to the time for the Daytona 500, he assumed Jonah, one of his
best friends from college, would be in town, so he followed his heart

65

and went for it. If it worked and he was able to find him, the friendship time alone would be awesome, even if Jonah decided not to contribute anything to the mission. This is the way Max's brain used to work. He used to have many spontaneous ideas with impulsive strategies that seemed to work. Even if they weren't all as grand as the Big Beef meeting just had been, they used to hit him every week, and sometimes every day. He texted Ray and told him he might be gone for the night. He had to visit another wealthy business friend in Daytona. If things worked out, it could be as lucrative or more so than Big Beef. He knew what the response was going to be, and it was, "It's about time."

The Richards girls jumped out of the van and rushed in to see Ray and Sally. Sally was a second mother to all of them, and they all loved her in that same way. Sally and Ray were never able to conceive any children of their own, so Max and his brothers were their sons, and Abigail and her sisters were their daughters. It was so great for all the kids to have a second set of parents in their lives who loved them, looked out for them, and challenged them to be the best they could be. And Sally was totally ready for them. No wonder she had stayed home from the airport. She had baked their favorite treats. She had decorated their rooms with old pictures and stuffed animals, and she had a mission polo shirt put out for each of them on their beds, in just their right sizes. Sally's heart was so full just seeing the girls all together as they got out of the van. When they rushed into the kitchen, almost tackling her with a group hug, there were many tears of joy and laughter.

Martha entered the kitchen just in time to see the emotional reunion and was amazed at the love and intimacy she witnessed. It really startled her in a good way. She was about ready to slip back into the living room so that she didn't interrupt it, when Ray came up behind her and asked her if she had any relatives she was that close to. She said she didn't but that it looked like something she would really, really like to have. Ray told her that as far as he and Sally were concerned, she did now. Martha gave the man she had only known for about 24 hours a huge, warm hug. She had a new aunt and uncle, as well. Finally, the girls let their aunt be free of arms, tears, and kisses, and they ran over to do the same with Ray. Martha moved out of the way quickly but desperately wanted to join the embrace.

Max decided not to call, text, or email Jonah that he was coming to see him. Jonah was the CEO of a surfing company that dabbled in many other areas of recreation, a Northwestern alum, and a former intramurals teammate and fraternity brother. They were really close friends at school, but neither man had done a great job of staying connected. Jonah had always been a free spirit, a trendsetter, an out-of-the-box thinker, doer, and liver. He had earned his MBA in a year and a half and started two companies by the time he graduated. From Florida originally, he moved back home and was probably a multi-millionaire already. Jonah might also be one of the nicest guys in the world. You wouldn't think a guy that smart, that successful, and that handsome could be that nice, but he was. And he was notoriously single, preferring to casually date, but never getting serious with any of the many women who were very interested. Jonah's parents had died when he was young, leaving him a product of the foster care system, and though he eventually found a great home with great parents, he had several experiences that were not pleasant, so he didn't mind telling you about his issues with the system. He also put his money where his mouth was with many donations to boys' and girls' homes along the Florida coast.

Max pulled into a Big Beef for a late dinner and Googled Jonah to find out where his main office was located. He also sent Jim a selfie of his enormous plate of food, which, Jim immediately replied, was on the house. Max didn't know how Jim would relay that to the restaurant outside of Daytona, but he knew that it was a done deal as soon as Jim texted. It was a great meal, and Max savored the steak and potato, letting himself eat at a relaxed pace. As expected, the waiter told him his meal was paid for by the company and he could leave whenever he wanted. Max left him a $20 bill and headed down to the business district. It took about ten minutes to find the place and just like he imagined, even though it was after 8:00 p.m., the offices of Smith Enterprises were lit up and active with people. He wasn't sure what he was going to do if that hadn't been true, but he was glad that he didn't have to worry about it. It certainly seemed that the favor of God was upon him on this trip. Everything that he thought of, planned, responded to, and passionately pursued was working out for him. Would that be the case with Abigail also?

He squeezed the VW into a tight parking spot and, with more energy than he should have had after a 12-hour work day already, he jogged across the parking lot and entered the building. JW Enterprises was the first and only name on the office marquee, and it looked as if they had taken over a majority of the three-story facility. JW stood for Jonah's Whale, a reference to the Biblical character, not an interesting last name. Jonah believed in miracles. He felt his life was one. He believed that though he had experienced life in the belly of a whale through the foster system, the Lord had a vision and a calling for him to make money and give to others, that he would be blessed and bless others. Like everything else Jonah had dreamed of, JW Enterprises was doing just that. Jonah liked being rich, but he also had a huge heart for helping the community. He was a force of nature and a polarizing figure. People seemed to either love him or hate him, but it really didn't matter to him. He was kind to everyone anyway.

Chapter 7

Max had barely made it through the huge glass doors of the entrance when he was confronted by an obnoxious and controlling office manager named Antonio. He grilled Max on his name, occupation, interest in Jonah, and intention for this late hour. Max tried to explain the nature of his "pop by," but Antonio was not buying the story. Max left his name and number and was ready to head out the door when he heard Jonah's booming voice down the hall. Before the office manager could stop him, Max darted past him – yelling Jonah's NU nickname, "J-Dog" – and the two athletic men nearly knocked each other over with their bro-hug embrace. Antonio retreated back to his corner vestibule disappointed that someone had eluded his control and containment, sad that he had not been the one to broker the reunion. Antonio adored Jonah and tried to please him always. Through his bulldog tenacity for the protection of the company, he was in line for a promotion soon.

Ray, Sally, Abigail, her sisters, and Martha had a two-hour meal full of food, love, joy, and laughter. It felt like the old days, and in such a short time, Martha felt like she belonged – almost like she was another sister and daughter. Abigail pulled Sally aside at a convenient moment and asked her why she hadn't told her Max was also coming to Florida when she called. Sally told her the story of the simultaneous contacts, and though the visits were related, they were also unrelated. The more important and selfish reason for the secrecy, however, was Ray and Sally desperately needed both of them this week to save the mission. She apologized, but Abigail got the distinct impression that Sally was not sorry and that she had another motive besides the mission. Sally also assured her that Martha's relationship with Max was platonic, at least for now, at least she thought so.

Max and Jonah spent hours catching up about life, work, love, and dreams at a beach club where everyone knew Jonah by name. Jonah always inspired Max and always told him the truth, just as Ray did, so when they started to talk about Abigail, Jonah became the fourth person to give Max an earful about his stupidity. He scolded him, challenged him, threatened him, and literally punched him, twice. He told Max that Abigail was such a quality woman that it made his own pursuit of a wife difficult because he compared all of the women he dated to her. That stunned Max, and for the second time that day he became a bit emotional. That changed from sadness to anger when Jonah added that if Max was truly done with Abigail, he was going to look her up and make his move. And he wasn't kidding. Max was shocked at this admission and heard the message loudly and clearly. Finally, as the men grew quiet and the hour slipped past midnight, Max asked Jonah what he had come to Daytona for in the first place – the gift for the mission.

Abigail watched the front door over and over again, though she tried to stop herself from doing it. She finally stopped around 10 p.m. when Ray remembered to tell Sally Max was not coming home because he was hanging out with his college friend, Jonah, in Daytona. Upon this announcement, everyone instinctively gazed at Abigail, and even though she tried not to react, she knew she was blushing. She forced a smile and a polite laugh and switched the attention by talking about how wonderful Jonah was. Every female in the room was disappointed Max wouldn't return to Cocoa that night, but they now imagined two handsome men rather than just one. The ladies eventually slowed down for the night and curled up with books in the living room. Around 11:30 p.m., Martha asked

Abigail privately if she could talk to her outside and Abigail nodded affirmatively. They slowly ventured onto the veranda while everyone else lowered their books and watched. Phoebe lightly put her book down on the seat beside her and started to get up to sneak a listen to the conversation, but Aunt Sally's stern look of disapproval returned her to her seat. This would be an interesting discussion, but one between Martha and only one of the Richards girls.

As was her spirit, Martha did not waste time on pleasantries or random topics of conversation once the two women were far enough away from the living room to secure confidentiality. She looked Abigail right in the eyes and asked if she could pursue Max. Abigail was stunned, turning away for at least 20 seconds. Though somewhat angry, she appreciated the candor and forthrightness. And what right did she have to stop Martha from Max? They weren't officially dating or engaged, and she had been the one to call it off, so what right did she have to block Martha from the hunt? Besides, maybe this was a way for Abigail to find out if Max had really moved on from her, though the surprise phone call certainly hadn't felt that way. Abigail turned back to face Martha, and after pausing longer than she had intended, gave Martha permission to pursue Max. But as the words, "That would be fine; we are not dating any longer or engaged, and Max is still a great guy" came out of her mouth, her voice cracked, and she had to immediately excuse herself from the veranda and go back into the house. Martha was wise enough not to head back into the room of the reading Richards sisters, but was smiling from ear to ear as she headed to her room via the back stairs. Abigail had a good cry with her sisters while they whispered about the audacity of Martha's bold request. Missy and Phoebe tried to console Abigail, but none of them knew Max well enough anymore to know whether he would have any interest in Martha – besides her obvious physical attributes – a thought that years before would not have entered any of their minds, especially Abigail's.

Chapter 8

Tuesday

Jonah woke Max up at daybreak to go for a run on the beach. Did that man ever get tired? They came back home, showered, had an organic breakfast, and headed off for a tour of the surfboard production site. Along the way, Jonah reiterated his challenge about Abigail and told Max he would give him a week to make up his mind before he would contact her to pursue a relationship with her. Max didn't know if he wanted to punch Jonah or hug him, but if his intent was to make Max wake up and pay attention to his heart and his future, it worked! And he also knew Jonah wasn't kidding. He would pursue Abigail hard, and Max was more than a little concerned Abigail might be interested. Jonah and Abigail were already friends and had spent a ton of time together at college. It wouldn't be a huge switch to move to a dating relationship, and Jonah would never take Abigail for granted the way Max had done the past four years. Max decided to text Abigail as they pulled into the parking lot. "Hope you have a great day" is all he said.

Ray and Sally had the plan for Tuesday laid out on the kitchen island along with the assignments, the fruit, the croissants, and the coffees. Martha and Phoebe were assigned to the merchants who had committed to the service day to finalize needs, details, times, and materials. They had about seven places to go and should be done by lunch. Missy was assigned to go with Sally to seek a couple of new merchants who had expressed interest in being part of the community day in the past but had not finalized any commitment, investment, or participation. Until three days ago, Sally and Ray had put those new possible merchants in the "maybe next year" file, but now that they had a full team of event-planning professionals in the house, they thought it was worth a shot. Besides, sometimes the urgency of the commitment leads to a quicker decision and a better chance for a successful partnership. Missy's PR background, effervescent energy, and knockout looks were also a big asset for a potential client. Sally would just be there for the details and the reinforcement of history, tradition, gratitude, and paperwork. It was amazing how much the youthful synergy was infusing Ray and Sally with more passion and spirit. Ray and Abigail were the last partners assigned together and they headed over to the mission business office to spend the morning organizing and uncovering the accounting books. Ray was weeks behind in the ledger, so Abigail knew she had a challenge ahead of her. She hoped she didn't find the mission in worse financial shape than what Ray had already reported, but she feared it might be the case.

Max was enthralled by the surfboard factory, so he was thrilled when, as they finished the tour, Jonah presented Max with a Heart and Soul Rescue Mission surfboard for the silent auction. The surfboard was not only super cool, with a hip and colorful style, but also of high quality, retailing for $1,200, so it would certainly garner top dollar at the banquet. Max couldn't believe Jonah had found the time to get that board ordered, let alone manufactured, between last night and this morning, but he wasn't really surprised and didn't even ask about it; he just thanked Jonah profusely, thinking in the back of his mind that he might have to buy it himself. Max tied the surfboard to the roof of the VW, while both men reminisced of their college days and trying to surf on Lake Michigan. The only times the waves were high enough to surf, when there was a huge storm blowing down from Wisconsin or the UP of Michigan, the beaches

were always closed. Thus, you had to break the law and risk your

life if you wanted to truly surf in Chicago, and the friends had taken

that risk more than once in their undergraduate days.

Jonah told Max there was one more place they had to visit

before he could head back to Cocoa, and there was no use

questioning Jonah or disagreeing with him when he was in his zone.

It was best just to go along for the ride – it was rarely anything less

than exceptional – and since the surfboard had already been a

fantastic surprise, Max couldn't wait to see what was next. The

whole morning, however, despite the amazing time he was having

with Jonah, Max kept thinking about Abigail and Martha. Though

he really missed Abigail, he was intrigued by Martha and wondered

what a dating relationship with another woman would be like.

Abigail sat down in Brad's old chair behind a beautiful

antique desk and sighed. There was a stack of files, papers, ledgers,

and payroll checks; it was a gigantic mess. Ray was at his desk across

the room and had already started responding to his e-mail, so Abigail

knew she was pretty much tasked with figuring it out on her own.

Her phone buzzed as she opened up her laptop and prepared to get her spreadsheet magic started. Glancing down and seeing Max's name and the text he had sent, she wondered what was going on. She had just told Martha she could pursue Max, yet now he was acting as if he were pursuing her again. But this wasn't pursuit as a boyfriend or fiancé; this was a friend's pursuit. Why, then, did it feel so good? It felt like a return to a simpler time, a time when the friendship was first and mattered most. Oh well, she didn't have the time to think too much about it. She had such a ton of work to do that she didn't even remember she was going to see Max later that day for the first time in almost a month.

Jonah gave terrible directions to Max. It seemed like he tried to get Max turned around or lost. Finally, after driving through downtown in a big square, Jonah told Max to park inside a large parking garage. Jonah instructed Max to head to the basement level, at least four turns down. They parked in an unmarked spot, and Jonah hopped out of the car, telling Max to join him. They followed the yellow path to the elevators and stairwell but didn't go through either of those doors. Instead, Jonah went to a service entrance door and, using a key, opened it. It was pitch black inside; Max couldn't see a thing. Jonah told Max to stay put and not to use his phone light until he turned on the lights before disappearing into the dark. Max told him not to worry; he couldn't see anything except Jonah's phone light and the path he took along a wall, which obviously led to the fuse box. With a click and a bang, suddenly the entire room flooded with powerful overhead and runway lights down each aisle, coming right to Max's shoes. Jonah had created a miniature Northwestern gymnasium, complete with a scoreboard, bleachers, and the purple N on the court. Jonah ran down to the court singing the NU fight song, beckoning Max to do the same. It was a good thing that Max had stayed put when ordered to by Jonah because right in front of him was a set of concrete stairs. It was much easier to run down them when he could see.

Everyone met back in Sally's kitchen for lunch, each with great news to report. Martha and Phoebe were able to secure final details with every single vendor on their schedule and even picked up one additional one – a chiropractor who was willing to donate five-minute head and shoulder massages. He would send three assistants with three chairs, which would likely be able to handle the flood of community members who would enjoy this service. That was something Ray had always wanted for the event but had never been able to secure before, and he announced that he planned to be the first recipient. Missy and Sally had even better news. With Missy's charm, spirit, and persuasion, four additional vendors had signed on for the Celebration with several silent auction donations as well. What had once been the smallest number of vendors for the annual celebration was quickly returning at least to normal numbers. Sally was beaming and nodding in affirmation and approval as Missy recapped their success. She had had so much fun watching Missy work. It reminded her of herself when she was that age. Missy was pretty sure one of the companies was going to make a sizeable donation also, but she wanted to let Ray – or maybe Max – take care of that piece of the puzzle.

Abigail and Ray also reported progress but were not quite as energetic or enthused as the other teams. Ray had not been able to help Abigail much at all, and after four hours of organizing, assessing, and evaluating, Abigail said she had at least two days left before she would feel good leaving it back in Ray's hands. Ray winked at her and said he thought he wouldn't take the job back after this week anyway – that she was just starting her takeover of the business side of the mission. Abigail laughed, knowing there was some truth behind the teasing, and admitted it was good to do some accounting that mattered to people beyond making money. She always liked accounting work, but she especially liked it when it involved missions, community, and people who really needed her administrative, financial, and accounting skills.

Max and Jonah played for an hour, worked up a great sweat, and enjoyed a couple of games of two-on-two with a couple of Jonah's other executives who just happened to show up around 8:00. They played almost daily at that time, Jonah said. It helped all of them stay in shape, stay open-minded, and sometimes their best ideas flowed out of one of their competitions. They posed for a picture to post on the Instagram account of one of the executives, tagging the four of them and then showered at the on-site locker room facility. But Jonah wasn't done with Max yet. He required Max to come back to JW's main office with him to show off a couple of new projects he was ready to launch. They had also ridden together, so either way, they were heading back to JW Enterprises. Every surprise Jonah had shown so far had been great, so Max sent Ray the picture of the four basketballers along with a message of his further-delayed arrival.

One of the new opportunities, Jonah shared on the ride back to the office, fit Max to a T, and he needed a new executive to lead it. Jonah let that sink in for quite a while, and the silence let him know he might have hit a soft spot in Max's career angst. Did he need a new job? A change of scenery? An opportunity to partner with a great friend was super appealing, and Max knew the money made would be just as good or better than his current salary at VanStevens. They parked in the CEO spot right in front of the building and bustled into the corridor where Antonio was waiting with smoothies and Jonah's schedule for the day. Max reflected on the morning while Jonah and Antonio walked through his day. Max had forgotten how fun it was to be around Jonah, to dream with him, to work on things that were his own creation. Antonio gave

Max a look of jealousy and consternation before the two friends and several other executives convened in Jonah's office.

Jonah put on an even harder sell for the vacant position at lunch. It was a flat-out job offer now. Jonah, Max, and three other VP's had spent two hours laying out a business plan for the new venture, with Max even taking the lead a few times regarding his specialties, marketing and sales. Jonah said he would give Max the same kind of package he currently earned, but with a 10% raise in his salary, stock options, and a percentage of product development rights so that Max had a stake in the venture that would be his forever. It was an amazing opportunity – Max was really honored and excited about it – but the thing that kept him from immediately accepting was Abigail. With his keen insight and discernment, Jonah figured the Abigail piece out by dessert and once again let Max know he better marry her and move down to Florida before it was too late. Besides, Jonah continued, maybe Abigail would move to Florida also, especially if she had a ring on her finger. Max said he wasn't sure if that was even an option anymore. Then, as Jonah paid for the meal, Max turned the tables on Jonah and asked him where his soul mate was. Jonah smirked and asked if Max meant Abigail, but then, in all seriousness, for the first time in 24 hours, Jonah was quiet, reserved, and reflective. He told Max that since he had become so successful, he couldn't figure out which women were interested in him and which were interested in his money and his toys. Max thought it wasn't much of a problem, but Jonah told him it was exhausting, and he was sick of it. He wanted to settle down – share his success with someone, raise a family, enjoy his work more – but he needed an assertive, bold, and confident woman who wasn't afraid to live on the edge. Before his description was even done, Max knew that Jonah had to meet Martha, and soon. It would move Martha out of his hair and onto Jonah's radar, and once Jonah had something on his radar, he normally finished the pursuit. And frankly, that seemed to be Martha's MO as well.

After lunch Abigail decided to text Max back. She deliberated with her sisters what to say and finally decided on a simple "Thanks, you too." They decided she should be appreciative but coy and not ask questions or give comments that might lead to more conversations unless Max did first. After all, they had the distinct advantage of knowing they were going to see Max that afternoon or evening. She wanted to talk to him again, but alone. She thought about taking a walk on the beach to catch up, hold hands, and talk about life. How desperately they needed to get some things out in the open. But what about Martha, who was in the picture now? The more time away from him and the more Martha pursued him, the more Abigail wanted to reconsider her decision. But had Max changed? Was he ready to truly commit to marriage and make their dreams a reality – finally? Without telling her sisters, she typed one more text. She stared at it for 20-30 seconds and then just left it alone and put her phone back in her jeans. It said, "I miss you."

The afternoon assignments were delivered, and Abigail had to admit Martha was not only fitting in with the Heart and Soul work ethic but also that she seemed to be a different person around her family, and especially Sally. Though the sisters were apprehensive about the Max piece of that equation, they were glad to have the help, and they began to enjoy her as a friend. Martha, for all of her flirting, hair tossing, and extreme feminism, was really a down-to-earth girl, who worked hard and said what she felt like saying. There was no need to guess or speculate with Martha. She was out there for all to see, and when you have to fit in with three sisters and a tight family, that is probably the best personality and temperament to have. Even Abigail admitted that once you got used to her style and brashness, Martha was kind of refreshing. Before they left, and in front of everybody else, Sally gave Martha a huge hug, told her how much she loved her, and welcomed her to stay as long as she wanted. Everyone knew Sally was not just saying that. She meant it, and she did it publicly on purpose. Like it or not, Martha was now a part of the family. Abigail prayed that Martha was not the future Mrs. Max McGovern.

As the girls paired off and prepared to head out the door, Sally's phone buzzed, and she greeted Max affectionately. "Yes, of course," she said as she ended the 30-second call with a huge grin. Everyone paused and fiddled around with their keys, phones, or shoes, waiting for Sally to inform them of the news. Finally Ray, exasperated, asked, "Well, what is it, Sally?" She informed them Max would be home by late afternoon, in time for dinner, and he had great news for the celebration. He also was bringing his friend Jonah Smith with him. And right as the beautiful girls walked to their cars, she shouted out to them what Abigail was about to tell them anyway – Jonah happened to be single, handsome, and rich. The girls all giggled as they set off to conquer their assigned duties, one of which was to come back by 4 p.m. to have some beach time before dinner, something all the girls had wanted but were afraid to ask for, so Sally had mandated the time in the afternoon schedule. How did Sally always seem to know what they needed and wanted without asking? What a special lady she was.

It took Jonah a few hours to get his executive team prepared for his absence. He was excited to take this break from the grind. He loved his work, and he made it fun for everyone, but it was still a lot of pressure and a lonely existence without a partner: a great friend or a wife or both. While Max waited for Jonah in the fancy lobby – which looked more like a health club – he stared out the window, watched the waves off the Atlantic, and thought deep and hard about his life. He would love to work with Jonah, get out of the cold, get away from city life, get back to being who he really was, who he had been, and who he wanted to be again. He was startled

out of his introspection by his phone. How nice it had been not to

have a constant flood of texts, emails, requests, demands, schedule

reminders, and urgent orders from work. He dreaded pulling the

phone out of his pocket, but he was delighted to be wrong about the

message. It was Abigail. It wasn't much of a text, but she had

responded. It was a start. He was pretty sure he still had a chance,

and he couldn't wait to take it, but he knew he had to take it slowly.

And, oh yeah, when would he even get to see her again?

Chapter 9

The girls were all back before 4:00, in their swimsuits, and off to the beach without even updating anybody about their duties. Only Abigail was not finished yet, and Sally knew that she would have to go over to the office and require her to leave. Abigail was such a hard worker, such a responsible woman. Sally was worried that she had forgotten how to have fun, how to be free and enjoy herself. Sally took Ray and Abigail some tea and then gave them each the 15-minute warning. She was coming back at 4:30 and the office was closing, no questions, debates, or comments allowed. Ray and Abigail knew better than to try to challenge the edict. They had made good progress today, but Abigail had found some more bad news financially that she didn't know how to bring up just yet. Did Ray even know? The Heart and Soul Rescue Mission was more than just behind. They were in debt, owed creditors a lot of money, and had started to get warnings and notices from the city, the investors, the credit card companies, and just about everybody else. Why had

Ray not even opened the letters? It seemed so unlike Ray not to face reality and attack it head on. There had to be more to the story.

Jonah and Max were on a road trip. It truly was like college – surf boards on top of the VW, luggage jammed into the back, windows open, music blaring. Max could easily see himself hanging out with Jonah regularly again and, man, that job offer was fantastic. Would his family understand if he took it and moved to Florida? Would Abigail? Would it be the final nail in his marital coffin, at least with Abigail? As they entered Brevard County toward Cocoa, Max knew they had about 30 minutes left and began to sell Martha to his friend. Jonah was intrigued. He listened. He asked questions. And of course, he wanted to know if she was beautiful. Max said she absolutely was, so Jonah asked if she were as beautiful as Abigail. Max paused for a moment and then said, "Not even close." The pause was all Jonah needed. He laughed and said appropriately, "I guess, we shall see, and I love redheads." Max replied, "Oh, you'll see alright."

Abigail caught up with her sisters and Martha as they waded and walked along the beach. It made Abigail long for the old days when life was simpler and easier. Could it be that way again? Abigail

snuck up behind them and kicked water all over their backs. The

girls squealed appropriately and then chased Abigail until she

jumped into the water for safety – and because she knew they were

going to throw her in anyway. The girls laughed and played in the

water and sand like kids. Abigail was the first one to be done and

headed to the public showers to clean off. The rest of the girls said

they would come soon and, like always, followed the natural leader

as they continued to laugh and sing and play. After about five

minutes, Martha, Missy, and Phoebe headed to the showers also.

They reached the "T" in the beach front. To the left was the public

parking lot, straight ahead was a strip mall area with a restaurant and

stores, and on the right were the public showers and an access gate

to the business district where the mission was located. The three

girls were about ready to take a right turn to the showers when, to

the left, two handsome and well-toned men appeared – Max and

Jonah.

Max wasn't shocked to see Martha on the beach, and he

tried not to stare at her well-shaped body in the swimming suit, but

Aunt Sally hadn't say anything about Missy or Phoebe. He was

shocked. He was thrilled. He was scared. He was sinking into the

sand dumbfounded when all the girls smiled and waved. But they

were also a mess. They looked at each other, eyed the two striking

men again, and immediately took off for the showers – laughing and

squealing along the way. It was Phoebe who finally turned and yelled

as she backpedaled that Abigail was here also. She was already in

the showers. Max and Jonah glanced at each other and laughed,

prompting Jonah to suggest that they both were now going to get a

chance to act on their convictions much more quickly than they had

thought. Max couldn't believe his fortune. He now had goose

bumps all over his body and his stomach was queasy. Could this day

possibly get any better? And how cool that Ray and Sally had all this

help for the mission.

Max shook his head, sighed, and took off toward the water,

so Jonah could throw him the football they had brought. There

wasn't any reason to stress or worry about the conglomeration of

friends and family descending on Cocoa Beach. His brother and the

band would be there in a day or two also, and he wanted to tell the girls. Furthermore, Max didn't care how much sand Martha was wearing; she looked amazing, and he knew Jonah had noticed.

Maybe that would get Max out of Martha's line of fire, and maybe Jonah would now focus on Martha instead of Abigail. He didn't know if it was Florida, the job offer, Ray and Sally, the rescue mission, or just being away from Chicago in the winter, but Max hadn't felt this good in months, if not years. Jonah ran down to join Max near the water and asked if he had a choice of any of the four women. Max knew Jonah was busting his chops again, but it didn't faze him this time. He was already making progress on his purpose. Max told him two of the girls were open for pursuit, and two of the girls were off limits. Phoebe was off limits because she was only 18, and Abigail was off limits because Max needed to give the relationship one more shot. "Fair enough," Jonah said. Martha and Missy were now in his crosshairs, both women fitting the personality profile he was looking for anyway.

The girls soon appeared again, all cleaned up from quick showers, but the men had delayed their intended return to the mission. They all ran down to the ocean, yelling and screaming, where Max and Jonah were throwing the football. Martha and Missy joined them, each girl an excellent athlete in her own right, having played multiple sports in high school. Phoebe and Abigail followed arm in arm, not far behind, but not close enough to get a ball thrown their direction. Abigail did not like sports much, though she attended the Northwestern games when in college, and Phoebe was a dance and drama girl. Unbeknownst to the kids, Ray and Sally sat on the veranda sipping some wine, watching the young and the restless frolic on the beach together. Their unofficially adopted children were mingling, laughing, flirting, and enjoying the beauty of the beach, each other, and the Florida sun. Quite obviously, Missy and Phoebe were interested in Jonah, but Martha and Abigail appeared to have their eyes and heart set on Max. The veteran married couple was quite entertained by the whole scenario and chuckled together at the hormones and communication involved. They both really wanted Abigail and Max to end up together, but they understood life and love enough to know the matches would work themselves out in due time. The two long-term love birds smiled at each other, leaning into each other shoulder to shoulder.

Chapter 9

After a few more minutes, Sally called them all in for dinner. She had been cooking for several hours, having not originally anticipated feeding eight people.

Chapter 10

There had not been a livelier and more entertaining dinner at Ray and Sally's since, well, since the Richards and McGoverns were last there all together about six years ago. Throw in Jonah and Martha – two more strong, beautiful, and assertive people – and the meal and the conversation were quite intense and spirited. Halfway through the lasagna, Missy gasped. She had totally forgotten to book the local band for the dance! Not to worry, Max told her; he had already booked his brothers and their band. They were driving the long way down to Florida from Chicago and should be there tomorrow or Thursday. The Richards girls all clapped at the news and launched into stories of the families vacationing together, including some seriously funny events that had taken place. Missy blushed slightly around the cheeks as she shared. She and Matt, the youngest McGovern son, had dated briefly the summer before they headed off to college. It didn't last, but it could have; they just had chosen not to commit to each other while at school. Subsequently, they both had serious relationships that didn't work out, but they had never lost their fondness for each other. Sally saw the look on Missy's face and made a note to herself to ask about Missy's reaction to the news of the McGovern Band making their music at the mission. Abigail also saw the look and knew the break-up story and the sadness behind it. She also knew Missy would have loved to have given the relationship a shot while they were in college, but went along with the break-up so that Matt wouldn't feel guilty. Her long-term relationship with Matt was positive, but Missy had told Abigail many times her heart had never totally recovered or moved on from him. This week continued to get more intriguing and interesting every day. The fact that it was the week of Valentine's Day made it all the more romantic.

Martha had made sure she sat next to Max at the meal and flirted and touched him as much as she could. It did not appear to influence or impress Max, but it still made Abigail cringe inside. Why did she tell Martha that Max was on the open market? Abigail made sure to direct comments, questions, and remarks Max's way during the meal, definitely catching his eyes on more than one occasion, but she also caught eyes with Jonah, who seemed to be paying a lot of attention to her also. And there was no doubt about it – Jonah was one fine looking man, but he reminded her of Martha. He was so bold, so confident. And he was very used to getting what he wanted. She hoped Jonah did not want to be with her, but it did feel good to think he might, or that he at least considered her an attractive person also.

Mike, Matt, and their bandmates decided to leave Tuesday night and drive all night. It wasn't the fun way to travel, but it was the quickest and saved them from having a night in a hotel, even though Max would have footed the bill. They had four drivers, each driving a four-hour shift, with music only allowed in ear buds so that everyone could make sure to get some sleep. As the rest of their siblings finished chocolate cake in Cocoa Beach, the McGovern Marauders, one of Chicago's best up-and-coming country bands, loaded up their two vans and headed south. They really hoped that this drive and diversion was worth it. They had just released their third CD so they brought a bunch of copies and hoped, at least, to sell a few and generate some new fans in the south. It wasn't that long ago that Max had been a member of the band, but he had dropped out when his job took off, and though the band had found another capable bass player, it hadn't been quite the same since. They were definitely going to make Max play a few songs with them at the dance. As they turned onto the interstate for the 18-hour drive, Matt, who was not driving the first shift, got a call from Max. Turns out, Max told them, Missy and Phoebe were also down in Cocoa Beach. This peaked Matt's interest, so his first question to Max was if she were still single. Max answered in the affirmative, adding that she was looking mighty fine. This certainly helped Matt's motivation for the long journey. It would be great to see her again, and having the six siblings all together was always a blast. Mike's wife Cindy had not made the trip, but Mike called her anyway to tell her the fascinating news. Then Matt called his mother and filled her in on the movements of the men she had raised. She acted as surprised and innocent as she could, but she couldn't wait to see all of the children together again.

After the cake and some more stories and laughter, the party moved outside to the veranda, but and Ray and Sally decided to watch a movie in their room. They loved all the company and conversation, but it was also pretty tiring, and they wanted to give the young people room to be, well, young. Missy and Phoebe decided to walk the beach, purposely attempting to leave Max and Abigail alone. They invited Martha, but she declined. Max was going to join them, but the girls told him it was a ladies-only walk.

In the next moment, Martha grabbed Max's arm with authority and asked him to walk with her to the convenient store about a mile away instead. Max didn't think he could say no without being rude, so that left Jonah and Abigail alone. Surely, one of his best friends would not move in on the love of his life while he was getting gum and snack food, would he? As Martha dragged Max to the sidewalk, he glanced back and saw Jonah give Abigail a big hug. Abigail's body twisted as she received the hug, and for a moment – just the right moment – she faced the direction of Max and Martha, locking eyes with Max. Max looked inquisitively in return. He sensed longing in Abigail's eyes, but was she longing for him or Jonah, Max wondered, until the surprisingly strong Martha tugged him into a faster-paced walk.

It's About Time

Jonah asked Abigail if they could talk for a while. It had been years since they had seen each other, let alone had a conversation; Abigail really didn't have a choice. Jonah's desire to communicate with her would be unabated no matter how hard she tried, so it was easier to just receive the invitation willingly. Talking to Jonah was fun, but it was almost a challenge to get a word into the conversation. He had so much passion, so much bravado. But Abigail's mind was someplace else anyway. As was the case when he talked with Max about Abigail, Jonah could see Abigail's eyes change when she talked about Max. He could see the tilt of her head. After they had caught up on all his business ventures, Jonah moved to his target point with Abigail. As he had done with Max, he lit into Abigail about the silliness of the break-up, demanding to know why they were not married and why they were pretending they weren't still crazy about each other. Abigail began to cry and admitted that, of course, Jonah was right, but she had called it off because Max had changed. He had lost his roots. His foundation was unstable. He had become full of himself and his toys. She apologized when she realized Jonah became a tad self-conscious about the toy comment, but he took note of its merit.

Martha kept the death grip on Max's arm all the way to the store. She told Max the past few days had been the best in her life since her parents had died. She just adored Max's aunt and uncle, and she choked up some and waxed eloquently about the influence Ray and Sally were having on her in such a short time. Max agreed there was something special about Ray and Sally, the Rescue Mission, and this community of people. Martha also said being with Abigail and her sisters also had been surprisingly wonderful. Watching and participating in the McGovern/Richards family vacation was seriously changing her life and her whole career aspirations. Martha really began to cry then, telling Max their surprise meeting on the plane couldn't have been a coincidence. Max agreed, admitted to her the meeting was obviously of the Lord, and expressed his surprise as well concerning how well all the ladies were getting along. Right before they reached the 7-Eleven, Martha turned to Max, grabbed him by the shoulders, and gave him a huge hug that lasted at least 10 seconds. Max thought for a moment she was going to kiss him. She thanked him for inviting her to be with his family and told him how great it was to see him and be with him again. She snuggled him so tightly the rest of the way to the store that it was hard for Max even to walk. In the store Martha was playful and flirtatious – anybody watching would have assumed they were a longstanding couple. Max didn't dissuade her from the relationship culture she was creating. It felt good to be with a woman again, to feel affection and desire.

When Missy and Phoebe came back to the veranda, Jonah and Abigail were relaxing silently in the chairs. The sisters, however, were not done with the night and convinced Jonah and Abigail to go to the club down the beach, which was playing 90's cover music, a favorite of all the sisters. Never one to turn down a good time, Jonah hopped off his chair, grabbed Abigail's arm, and followed the girls back to the beach before Abigail could give any of the handful of excuses she had quickly prepared for why she couldn't go. Jonah texted Max as they walked with an invitation to him and Martha to meet them at Cheaters, a dance club on North Atlantic Avenue. Max didn't know if he should be excited or frightened by the invitation to go dancing, but Martha was ecstatic and made the decision for both of them. Max found the name of the club highly ironic as he and Martha made their way there, arm in arm. Three blocks ahead of them, Jonah and Abigail also strolled arm in arm to Cheaters. This was going to be an interesting night of dancing.

Chapter 11

When Max and Abigail were in high school and college, they had loved to dance. Music was such a huge part of the McGovern family, and dancing was a required talent, as well. So, it wasn't that Max didn't want to go to the club – it's that he wanted to dance with Abigail, but with Martha and the sisters there, he was going to have to dance with everybody. Cheaters was so crowded by the time Max and Martha arrived that it took them a while to find any of their family. They spotted Phoebe first at a stand-up table in a back corner, the only one she could find open, she told them. Missy was dancing nearby with some man no one knew. Max couldn't see Jonah or Abigail anywhere close. After a few minutes, "Take My Breath Away," the love song from *Top Gun*, came on, which beckoned many people to dance floor, including Jonah and Abigail, whom Max finally spotted. Max immediately broke out in a cold sweat as he saw Jonah and Abigail – her arms around his neck, his arms around her waist. They weren't body to body, but it was awfully close. Max wanted to run out on the floor and push Jonah aside, but before he could do anything stupid or impulsive, Martha put him in the arm bar again and marched him right out on the floor and right next to Jonah and Abigail.

After the movie, Ray couldn't sleep. Sally had fallen asleep during the movie, as she always did, and Ray had heard the kids come on and off the veranda, but it wasn't their talking that kept him awake. It was the realization that the mission was in deep financial trouble. He had known it for a while and honestly been in denial. He waited for the donations to come in and for Brad to come back with the $10,000, but a week turned into a month and he had to face the facts and make some decisions pretty quickly. He finally decided he had to wake Sally up and tell her the truth, the deep truth, about the mission's finances – right now. He couldn't hold it from her any longer, even with all the kids with them for the week. Sally wasn't surprised and wasn't mad, but she was very disappointed that Ray had not told her the extent of the issue earlier. He apologized but admitted he hadn't known the whole truth until he went back over to the mission after Abigail had opened all the mail and balanced the books. They were about $150,000 behind and running a monthly loss of over $2,000. Sally didn't really care about how it happened or what mistakes were made, by Ray or by Brad. What she wanted to know was what they were going to do about it. Ray didn't know for sure, but he knew his days of running the mission were almost over, and he really hoped Max would become the new executive director and soon.

Max had never been so uncomfortable on the dance floor before. He was slow dancing with Martha right next to Jonah slow dancing with Abigail. Something was terribly wrong with the picture, and then it got worse. Max tried to be respectful of Martha and to look at her once in a while as they swayed to the music, but not long enough to give her any intimacy. Then, out of the blue, Martha leaned forward, twisted Max's face to match hers, and kissed him – having waited until Abigail was facing their direction, unable to miss the event. Max was stunned, but he didn't pull away right away either, which made it worse. Abigail, shocked, viscerally responded by shoving herself away from Jonah, yelling Max's name out in disgust and pain, and running off the floor and out the door.

Max was furious with Martha and scolded her for the kiss as calmly as he could without making more of a scene than Abigail's departure had already created. Martha apologized but told Max she thought that he was interested in her, too. She started to explain – the airport club, inviting her to Cocoa, spending significant time with her once she was there – but Max was too flabbergasted to say anything other than though he liked Martha as a friend, his feelings for Abigail were not gone. If anything, they were back and stronger than ever. Max looked at Jonah with an unspoken request for back-up, so Jonah came over and offered to dance with Martha. Unfazed by anything that just occurred, Martha gave a significantly flirtatious and enthusiastic yes to Jonah's request, allowing Max to hurry out of the club and back to Ray and Sally's. He doubted Abigail would want to talk to him, but he had to try, at least. Martha was the first girl he had ever kissed besides Abigail, and he was positive that he wanted her to be his last. Melissa and Phoebe didn't witness the kiss. They just assumed Abigail was tired and had gone back to Sally's to go to bed. Neither Jonah nor Martha wanted to tell them either. They were having too much fun. Jonah saw the kiss, however, loved it, and was super impressed with Martha's gumption.

That was a bold and aggressive move, even if she had been wrong, or maybe slightly wrong, regarding Max's interest. That is the kind of woman Jonah was looking for. Jonah danced with all three ladies for another hour, saving the last two slow dances for Martha, the two unafraid to stare deeply into each other's eyes. Paying the waitress for the night's drinks, Missy and Phoebe giggled as they saw the obvious fire kindling between their two friends.

Chapter 12

Wednesday

Abigail went right into Aunt Sally's bedroom just as she had done as a teenager and threw herself on her bed. Ray and Sally had not gone back to sleep yet after Ray's financial confession, so Ray just moved over, then crawled out of bed and went downstairs to let the ladies have their bonding. Abigail told Sally the whole story, and though Sally was compassionate and empathetic, she told Abigail neither Max nor Martha had done anything wrong. Abigail was taken aback her mentor didn't recognize the obvious betrayal, but after trying to refute Sally's logic, Abigail finally had to admit that Sally was right. Abigail had told Martha Max was free and available. Max had invited Martha to come to the mission, long before Max knew Abigail would also come for a visit. Abigail had ended the relationship with Max. Max hadn't made that decision, though one could easily argue Max had encouraged the move through his passivity and indifference. It also seemed Martha was the aggressor and Max the receiver of the kiss. Not that this mattered much, but it was part of the equation.

Abigail finally relented her claim of injustice and instead settled on sulking.

But how was Abigail supposed to consider taking Max back again after that kiss? Sally said the kiss and her response to it should tell her everything she needed to know about how she still felt about Max. And how did Abigail know how Max felt about the kiss? She didn't, but that was not her primary concern. Sally continued to guide Abigail's wounded soul. It was Abigail's responsibility to tell Max how she felt about the kiss with Martha and how she felt about him, as well. Abigail left the room after about an hour of counsel, challenge, and wisdom, reminded again of how thankful she was to have Sally in her life. She wasn't ready to talk to Max yet, but she did feel much better about what had happened and what she eventually needed to do – even if Max and Martha started dating and eventually married. She wasn't normally an extremist in her responses to life, but the only man she had ever truly loved might have slipped through her fingertips, and that led to some dramatic swings in mood and behavior. Abigail went into her room, needing to talk to someone whom she loved and trusted, someone not here in Cocoa Beach. She called Stephanie. She needed to walk through the soap-opera day with her best friend.

Max ran home but did not catch Abigail before she went into Aunt Sally's room; Sally was a wiser option for her right now than he was anyway. Ray was watching Sports Center and motioned for Max to join him in the living room. Max grabbed a water out of the fridge and plopped down beside his uncle. He was still sweating from the run home. Ray asked Max to explain why Abigail burst into his room in tears five minutes ago. The news of her broken heart actually relieved Max; it was far better than a reaction of anger from Abigail. Ray laughed when Max reached the kiss part of the story and couldn't stop laughing. He said he knew he liked Martha and this 100% confirmed it. Max was startled by Ray's casual and obvious enjoyment of the response. Ray reminded him he and Abigail were not dating and that Martha was a beautiful and smart woman who saw an opportunity and took it. What was wrong with that? He also told Max he could learn a thing or two from Martha's spirit. She didn't over plan. She didn't mind change. She took advantage of opportunities right where they were and right when they came. Martha had suffered great losses and through her grieving had recognized the need to fully embrace life, not waiting or cowering in fear or trepidation. Maybe potentially losing Abigail, Ray continued, though certainly not as devastating as Martha losing her parents in a car crash, had awakened Max's heart to the truth about love and commitment issues that would help him embrace life. Max had finished his water and wiped off his sweat and was now leaning forward to soak in Ray's wisdom. Max thanked Ray for the truth, as always, and headed out to the veranda and down to the beach to ponder his life and talk to the Lord in a sincere way for the first time in years.

Now that Max thought about it, he guessed Ray was right, but would Abigail blame him for the kiss and think he no longer was interested in her? He had to talk to her soon, but he and Ray had agreed tonight was probably not the right time. Max had a super busy day tomorrow – a meeting with Reginald and Felipe's sons and some other final details with the city council. Then, by mid-afternoon, his brothers would arrive, and they would need to start setting up all the tables, chairs, platforms, stage, sound equipment, and the outdoor vendor tents. It would be a 12-hour day of hard work and preparation, so a deep conversation with Abigail in the midst of all of that was not likely going to happen. But every day now was going to be packed until they had to leave for Chicago again, so when would he get a chance? He sighed, grabbed another water, and started to turn to go back in the house when his cell phone buzzed. Who could it be at this hour? It was almost 1 a.m. He hoped it was Abigail, but when he checked the ID he was shocked and scared, and he hesitated to answer.

Fred VanStevens had only called Max this late on one other occasion and not for a good reason. Four years ago, VanStevens Inc. had lost a client of seven-figure significance, and though Max hadn't done anything particularly wrong with that client, Fred had still assigned him to fly immediately to Italy to solve the problem. It took Max almost three months to restore the relationship, secure the client again, and set up the marketing infrastructure necessary to not have to worry about that contract again. His diligence had earned him a ton of respect, admiration, and affirmation from Fred and his colleagues, but it had cost him the second anniversary date for his marriage to Abigail. He had blatantly chosen his work over Abigail, which hadn't really dawned on him, to this extent, until this exact moment, four years later at 1 in the morning. Would he have to do it again?

Fred apologized profusely for the call, explaining he planned on just leaving Max a voice mail message, for it was too long for a text. He never expected to talk to him at that moment, but, nevertheless, he was glad he had Max's ear and needed ten minutes of his time. Max considered saying he didn't, in fact, have the time. He didn't even know if he wanted to work at VanStevens any longer, and he didn't really care what financial emergency required his attention at 1 in the morning. However, since he was teetering on being fired already and hadn't made any commitment with Jonah about a possible new venture, he simply said, "Yes, sir."

The largest international client in VanStevens' stable was the French company Charpentier (Carpenter) in Paris. Fred had secured the contract himself about 30 years ago, and it was now worth well over $2 million a year to VanStevens. Max listened, confused – he had not worked with Charpentier before – but you don't interrupt your boss for minor details, so he kept walking and listening. The Charpentier contract was at the Vice President level. No one else handled any of it except the executives. In light of Fred's having made Max take a week off to find himself (or lose his job), the request Fred made next blew Max's mind completely.

Fred wanted Max to leave for France immediately, or at least tomorrow morning, to spend a couple of months with Charpentier's VP of Marketing, learning the ropes of this level of work. Fred apologized to Max for allowing him to be bored and restless at VanStevens and not realizing sooner he needed new challenges, a new mountain to climb. Max, shocked, listened in complete silence as Fred continued. There would be a large promotion, a new corner office, his own secretary, an extra week of vacation, more stock options, and a bonus of at least $100,000 each year. But it had to start now; he didn't have time for Max to finish either grieving Abigail or enjoying his vacation.

Max finally uttered a few words of appreciation, probed some minor questions of detail and process, and asked Fred why he needed Max specifically for this role in France. Fred gladly told Max he needed someone not only loved adventure but also was great with people, great in other cultures, not afraid to outwork everybody else, committed to the company, flexible, and spontaneous. Max asked if he could please have until morning to decide. This was a massive decision and a massive opportunity, and he would at least like six hours to sleep on it. Fred did not like the delay but said he would call Max later that morning at 8:00 a.m. Florida time. "And Max," Fred said directly, "it's either France tomorrow or I am letting you go. Neither of us wants to see you work in the same position or in the same manner any further." Ending the call with Fred, Max was more confused than ever about his life and his feelings for Abigail, Martha, VanStevens, Jonah, Chicago, and Florida. He was a big mess. He strolled back to the mission in an almost catatonic state and went straight to bed.

Chapter 13

Neither Abigail nor Max slept much that night, and the Valentine's Day celebration and the mountain of work needed to make that event a success didn't cause the restlessness. Abigail tossed and turned and ruminated over her relationship with Max, as she had for the past three months, but somehow this time it was much different. After Martha's kiss with Max last night, it seemed her final decision – for keeps – needed to happen soon, really soon. For Max, he had received two amazing job offers in the same day, both including huge promotions, with the unexpected bump in salary, stocks, and status, not to mention the perks. He asked the Lord why He had given him two amazing opportunities, with all the incredible financial blessings attached, when he had hardly been a loyal son to the Heavenly Father? He had spent the past year, maybe even two years, being lazy, complacent, arrogant, and unmoved in compassion or by community. He recognized his need to return to the Lord, to a life of full passion and full commitment, and he knew, without a doubt, this conviction included Abigail as his wife. But did she feel the same way? Should he hop on the noon flight to Paris or say yes to Jonah and move to Florida? Neither awesome new venture guaranteed any time, touch, or marriage with Abigail. If he said yes to Paris, he realized it truly might be the end of the Max-and-Abigail dream. He wasn't sure he was good with that, yet he didn't know Abigail would give him another chance regardless. And if he said yes to Jonah, would Abigail consider moving to Florida, away from her family and away from the job she loved? How could such great opportunities cause such great stress?

Max left his room at 6:00 a.m. Florida time. He still had two hours before the call would come from Fred, and he knew whom he wanted to talk to about these choices in front of him. It wasn't Ray, though he was sure Ray would give him good advice. No, this time he wanted some non-family members who knew him well enough to tell him the truth in love. He knew where to find Reginald and Felipe. They always ate breakfast at the Pink Flamingo Diner, the worst-decorated restaurant in the city, but the one that had the best pancakes in town. The diner was another reminder to Max the outside doesn't always determine the inside. Though he knew the principle from his marketing studies, he didn't always remember it in his heart. Max found Reginald and Felipe in their normal booth, and they didn't act surprised to see him at all. They told him to pull up a chair, ordered him the unhealthiest item on the menu, and said they were glad he had come. Felipe launched into an apologetic about Felipe Jr. and the company, and Max realized his friends thought he had come to talk about his visit with their sons later that day. It took him five minutes to change their perception of his visit and to turn their attention to a topic they liked even better than work, love – more specifically, Abigail and love.

Abigail decided she didn't care about the kiss, well, at least not as the most important thing. What she needed to know was whether Max had changed or not, and she wasn't sure yet. It seemed as if maybe he had, but it took a couple of years for his uninterested and uncommitted side to show itself before. Could he shift back to the Max she knew and loved in a few weeks? Abigail woke both her sisters up – to their chagrin – needing some soul time, for who knew the history of the Max-and-Abigail saga better than they? When Abigail called and woke up Stephanie at 1 in the morning last night, her best friend had pretty much sided with Sally, asserting neither Max nor Martha had done anything wrong. Stephanie also agreed Abigail was obviously still very much in love with Max and needed to tell him soon. Once Abigail told Missy and Phoebe about the kiss, both girls perked up significantly, and Abigail had to stop Missy from walking into Martha's room and giving her a piece of her mind. This was the kind of unconditional love and loyalty Abigail needed. Abigail knew she was blessed beyond measure with her family, and sometimes it is good to bring your sisters into your business, all of your business.

Max spent ten minutes spilling his soul, and Reginald and Felipe sure enjoyed the dramatic night. They smiled and laughed and gave Max all the attention and focus he needed. He felt affirmed before they even gave him their two cents' worth on the life and love wisdom they had earned through difficult but well-lived lives. When Max finished his story, Felipe made it perfectly clear neither he nor Reginald was going to make the decision for him. That established, Felipe asked a question that penetrated a lot of the noise and brought some melody to the dissonance in Max's soul. Felipe asked Max what the most important thing in his life was. Max stammered and

stuttered and then had to shut up for a minute to really process and

communicate. He finally said that though his life didn't necessarily

show it of late, it was definitely love: God's love, his family's love,

and Abigail's love. Tears ran down Max's cheeks as he expounded

upon the blessings in his past, the blessings of this moment, and the

two amazing opportunities sitting at his feet. Max looked at them

for more specific questions or directives, but the two men remained

silent for a minute, sipping their coffees. Then Reginald gave Max

what should have been an easy next step to take if he were thinking

clearly. He suggested, with a twinkle in his eyes and a huge smile on

his face, that maybe Max should talk to Abigail about the Florida

and Paris options, to see how she felt about them before he made

any decision. Felipe continued the encouragement, reminding Max

he didn't have to be dating her to get her opinion, to hear her heart.

She had been his best friend for more than half his life. He told

Max, with even more passion, "If you are terrified about how she

will respond to these life-altering decisions, then why not ask her

ahead of time before you decide?" Max sat there amazed at the clarity of their direction. Felipe continued, "I think you have about 40 minutes to find her and listen to her, so you better get moving!"

Max couldn't believe the simplicity and clarity of the suggested next steps. He thanked the men several times, giving them a couple of hearty handshakes before dropping a $50 bill on the table. He knew they wouldn't take it, but he also knew they would leave it for the waitress. He texted Abigail on his way out the door, asking if they could please talk immediately and before 7:45. He would explain the urgency later, was on his way back to the mission, and would see her soon. He started to run, but when he reached the street, he decided against it. No need to sprint back frantically and get himself in a stressed-out and hyper mood. He would put his trust back in the Lord to lead him and his decisions. And he trusted Abigail to hear his heart and help him process his own soul, even if she never wanted to date him again. He was sure of that. He was sure of her.

Abigail and her sisters had gone for a walk on the beach to deconstruct the kiss incident from the night before without waking up the house. They analyzed the event from about five different perspectives before heading back to the mission. The sisters determined three realities based on the past 24 hours. One, Abigail still loved Max and was not ready to break it off forever. Two, Max was in a difficult time in his life and needed her friendship, if nothing else, to help him return to the man he was capable of becoming, regardless of whether she married him or not. And three, she needed to talk with Max sometime today, even with the chaotic schedule, to come to some peace about last night and some agreement about the immediate future. The girls entered the kitchen from the veranda, feeling good about their sister talk. Sally had prepared a typical hearty breakfast spread, as the girls ate, she asked for an update on Abigail's heart. Before Abigail could reply, her phone vibrated. The sisters and Sally hunched over Abigail's shoulder to see who it was. It was Max! She read the text to all of them and they squealed. Abigail didn't ask any of them for affirmation this time. She quickly answered yes, and then she and her sisters ran upstairs to get her ready.

Max and Abigail had agreed to meet at the business office of the mission at 7:15. That gave them at least 30 minutes to talk before the phone call, which wasn't enough time to cover his or their entire future but certainly would cover his immediate dilemma. Abigail didn't know the urgency of the time frame, but she was fascinated by Max's hyper energy and frenetic pace. That was the way he was when he was operating in a good place, a healthy place, a holy place. Whatever it was Max wanted to talk about, Abigail was thrilled to hear it and to observe the old Max coming back. To Max, it didn't matter how Abigail responded to his disclosure and communication; he was just thrilled she had agreed to meet him, and he sensed she was not going to hold the Martha kiss against him for eternity.

There was another relationship meeting scheduled that morning, this one at 7:00, but it wasn't about business decisions. Martha and Jonah had decided to meet for a jog before breakfast. It didn't matter if Jonah had ten hours of sleep or three, he didn't alter from his fitness and health regimen, and Martha was more than willing to get up and run with the good-looking millionaire. Besides, she didn't have to tell him she hated mornings. She was a flexible and adaptable woman. If Jonah loved mornings, and their relationship grew and developed, she would figure out a way to love mornings also. She had made a move on Max last night that didn't work out, but she had moved on and was ready to make a move on Jonah today. It wasn't personal – it was love and romance, and there were two handsome, single men, great guys who needed wives. She was more than happy to oblige one of them, knowing they needed her every bit as much as she needed them.

Max was more nervous for this talk than he was for any presentation, project, pitch, or speech he had ever made, and this time, he did not have time to write it out, practice it, or polish it. He would bare his heart and soul at the Heart and Soul Mission. How fitting. This presentation was to the person who knew him best, whom he could never fool. If he didn't deliver from his most authentic and intimate place, she wouldn't buy it; she would know it was posturing and positioning, and she would be done with him – now, and probably forever. As Max approached the mission, he had to pass by one of the beach access points. When he came around the corner, there were Jonah and Martha, wearing about $400 worth of athletic gear and matching JW visors, on their way to the beach.

Max was glad to see them, especially together. Martha apologized for the kiss and said she and Jonah ended up talking into the middle of the night. They seemed so happy together already, so willing to give the relationship a chance right away. Relieved on many levels, Max marveled at both their spirits. He told them his plans with Abigail. Jonah smiled broadly, and Martha let out a loud girlish squeal of anticipation and joy. Max could tell how truly happy both Jonah and Martha were for him. It meant a lot to him, he told them. Then, spontaneously, Max gave each of them a big hug and a kiss, first Jonah and then Martha. He hadn't been this happy and determined in a long, long time.

Abigail was in her room with her sisters as they tried to pick an outfit that said, "I am still very interested, but you make me really mad sometimes, and I am not sure I trust you," but no one she knew marketed that kind of fashion. She settled on one of the combinations the girls had packed for her back in Chicago. Missy and Phoebe prepped Abigail as if it were her wedding day, except they only had ten minutes to finish their effort. Once they were satisfied with their sister's look, they invited Sally to come in and pray over Abigail for some extra peace and favor. Right after the

prayer, they heard a loud squeal. When Abigail ventured onto the

second-floor vista, she saw Max and Martha, for the second time in

12 hours, engaged in a kiss, and this time Max looked to be the

aggressive one. Neither Max nor Martha saw Abigail, so when her

sisters asked her who or what had made the noise, she kept the

observation to herself and told them it was nothing before bolting

out of the room.

Chapter 14

Max entered the office around 7:00 a.m., fifteen minutes early, which he hoped would impress Abigail because Max had a tendency to run late. (Of course, Abigail did not run late.) Ray was already in the office and working diligently at his desk. Everyone was up so early after a night when nobody enjoyed much sleep – so much pressure on all of them, so many deadlines, so many decisions to be made. Ray asked Max what he was doing there so early, and Max informed him of his breakfast meeting with Reginald and Felipe that precipitated the arranged meeting with Abigail. Ray said it was fortuitous that Max was there before Abigail because Ray had something really important to talk with Max about regarding his future. Max didn't know whose future Ray was referring to, his or Ray's, but Max told him he was glad to hear it. As soon as Abigail showed up, though, he would have to focus his attention and time on her because he had a work call coming in at 8:00. Ray said he understood.

Abigail went down to the kitchen alone, but her countenance had definitely changed. The sisters followed and commented that something was obviously wrong, hinting the source of the change in her countenance had been precipitated by what she had seen from the vista. Missy said it looked like she was wearing her tax season accountant's face. Still planning on meeting Max, Abigail tried to maintain her composure as she stomped around the kitchen and tried to put cream cheese on her bagel. But when her plastic knife broke, the dam burst, and the tears overflowed. She kicked the island frame, yelled something incomprehensible, and ran back to her room. Missy and Phoebe looked at each other in shock, Sally running in to join them from the living room, but none of them had any notion that could explain Abigail's sudden change in demeanor. They didn't have to wait long for an answer; in a few minutes Abigail texted her sisters, who obediently marched up to her room. The ladies were appropriately flabbergasted and unbelievably mad at what Abigail had observed. They couldn't believe it. How could Max kiss Martha again? And on his way to meet Abigail? Was he a two-timer? A cheater? Had he cheated on her in the past? All three girls were emotional and worked up this time, increasing each other's level of crisis without boundaries or reason. Thankfully, Sally had meandered toward the room and, overhearing the chaos, knocked strongly on the door.

Jonah and Martha proceeded to the beach, holding hands. Jonah had already started another recruiting plan, and he shared with Martha the idea of working for him, becoming the official interior designer for JW Inc. – or, if not that, at least moving to Orlando for her home base as a stewardess. He had a way, he told her, of helping people's dreams come true. Being with Jonah on the beach was already like a dream come true, Martha added, and the two began their bonding for life. Jonah also informed Martha of his recruiting pitch to Max, but Martha said she didn't think Max would take any job that took him farther away from Abigail. Jonah and Martha were not patient or planning people, so this romance was going to be fast and furious, either ending up in a quick marriage or a fast and messy failure. Either way, both were excited and willing to see where it led. They were two impetuous and driven people.

Ray told Max to sit down, a hard task for Max considering what was coming in about 10 minutes, but he did so out of his love and respect for his uncle. Ray then dropped a bombshell on Max, telling him that he was retiring as executive director of the mission at the end of May. It was about time he slowed down and enjoyed some years and travels with Sally before they were too old to be free with their choices. He winked at Max when he said it was about time, but then he really shocked Max with what followed. He told Max that he wanted Max to be his replacement and to take over by May. He had prayed about his replacement for years and every time the voice of the Lord spoke in a soft and quiet reflection, his mind led him to Max. Max asked about Sally, and Ray confirmed Sally agreed also. Of all their friends, family, and colleagues, Max had the right combination of gifts, heart, spirit, and skills. It just made sense. Furthermore, they were going to ask Abigail to be the new business officer for the mission – not in order to orchestrate their eventual marriage but because they were the two family members whose hearts and souls matched the heart and soul for the Heart and Soul Mission! It sounded really corny, but it was true, Ray affirmed. Max was super humbled by the declaration and confession of the Lord's leading. But why in the world would God give him three amazing job opportunities in the last 18 hours? How was he supposed to make sense of all this?

Sally told the girls to quit their whining and complaining, stifle the extra critical spirit regarding Max, leave their cell phones in their rooms, and follow her. They followed her down the stairs and out the front door. They would have followed her anywhere anyway, but Sally's disposition was not soft and cuddly at the moment. She was borderline irritated with them and it showed. Sally told them to get into the mission van and they drove off towards downtown with the three sisters wondering where they were headed and when the last time was they had gone anywhere in public without being totally put together first. Sally drove in silence, a stern and maternal look on her face. When in five minutes they pulled up to a woman's shelter, Sally told the girls they were going to help serve the breakfast. The girls obeyed exiting the van single file into the shelter. The building, rundown on the outside, was missing bricks and mortar, had cracked and boarded windows, and was littered with graffiti all over. The inside was in even worse shape. Twenty or 25 women waited in a line that worked its way into the hallway. Sally hugged every single one of them on her way to the kitchen, apologized for being late, and then introduced her "adopted daughters/nieces" to the entire group.

Max looked at his phone often as Ray finished his dream for the future of the mission, becoming more nervous and anxious with each passing view. First, 7:15 came and went, as did 7:20 and 7:25. Ray became aware of the time issue also, and both he and Max agreed this was not like Abigail. Surprise turned into worry when Abigail did not answer her phone. Finally, at 7:30, Ray and Max walked over to the house to look for her but didn't find anybody home. Sally, Abigail, Missy, Phoebe, Jonah, and Martha were all gone and the sisters' cell phones were in their rooms. It was pretty eerie. The men laughed about a possible rapture, but then wondered why they were both still there. Walking to the beach, they eventually ran into Jonah and Martha, who said they had not seen any of the other ladies. Jonah and Martha were walking hand in hand and looked like they had been a couple for years, as if they were simply headed for paradise. It was almost 7:50 now, and Max was a mess.

He went back to his room for the phone call and Ray said he would

drive down to the women's shelter and see if he could at least find

Sally. That was where she should be. He told Max he would text

him if he found her and she knew anything.

Three job offers in 18 hours – that had to be some kind of

record – two in Florida and one in Paris with an eventual return to

Chicago. All three used his gifts, talents, and abilities well, but one

paid substantially less than the other two. And yet, Max knew that

one would fulfill him the most. Working with Jonah would be the

most fun. Working as an executive with VanStevens would be the

most consistent and stable, and he did love to travel. Working at the

mission would be the hardest with the fewest guarantees about

anything. It was 7:59 when the phone rang, but it wasn't Fred. It

was Ray. He said he had found Sally and the girls. They were all

working at the women's shelter serving breakfast. When Ray asked

Abigail why she hadn't shown up for her meeting, she said she had

changed her mind about meeting with Max today and didn't want to

talk with him anymore until the week was over – maybe some time back in Chicago in March or April. Ray told Max that he was so sorry. He could feel the hurt in the silence on the other end. Max was heartbroken and threw the phone down on his bed. Ten seconds later, the phone rang again.

Chapter 15

Abigail and her sisters received the non-verbal message from Sally loudly and clearly. Exhausted from the two-hour breakfast shift and the half hour clean-up, Abigail reflected out loud that Sally normally did that whole serving shift on her own. They all shook their heads in confirmation and appreciation of Sally and her work ethic. Far removed now from their emotional meltdown about Max and Martha, they had been reminded that serving others is a great way to get the focus off yourself and your own drama. Waiting patiently outside for Sally to take them home, they hadn't missed their phones or their designer clothes. They reminisced about past trips to the mission, road trips to Disney World and Sea World, and getting sunburned on the beach. They also discussed what had to be done the rest of the day. Missy was creating a new website with an on-line donation option, an interactive opportunity to sign up for serving opportunities, and a place to watch highlights from this weekend's Valentine's Day Celebration. Phoebe was in charge of the decorations – this year they really wanted to go all out – so she and Sally were headed to Wal-Mart for a shopping spree. Abigail was destined for an afternoon back in the office with Ray. Sally finally appeared, looking fresher than any of the much younger women, and told them, with a gleam in her eye, it was time to go home and get ready to really work.

Abigail made it into the office around 10:30, still without her phone. She apologized to Ray for being late, promised to get a lot done, and sat in Brad's chair, which was starting to feel like her own. Before Abigail had to bring up the financial issues she had uncovered, Ray introduced the topic. He explained to Abigail what had happened and how, for the first time in his 35 years at the mission, he didn't have the answer, the energy, or the desire to tackle the financial problems. Ray continued by sharing he was going to retire in May, and he and Sally planned to travel. Abigail was stunned, but the shock increased greatly with Ray's next request. He wanted Abigail to become the business administrator for the mission, which included a reasonable salary and an opportunity to live in their home for free until she found her own place. Besides, he said, they would be gone so much, it would feel like her own home. Abigail offered a couple of silly excuses for why it might not be a wise move, but most of them were just fear and processing. She told Ray she would honestly consider it, but it certainly mattered who the executive director would be. Ray told her up until about three hours ago he thought it was going to be Max. But as of about 8:15, he was now open to recommendations and, if need be, a regional search. When Abigail asked Ray as casually as she could what Max had said when he turned the job down, Ray replied that it primarily had to do with an order from VanStevens for Max to be in France immediately. Max had left for the airport at 8:10, would be in Chicago by noon and in France by tonight, and would be gone for at least three months. Max had accepted a new position with his company with a big promotion. Ray then asked Abigail why she had skipped the arranged meeting with Max at 7:15.

Abigail immediately backpedaled and sat down, too stunned to even answer Ray's question. Max hadn't changed. The glimpses of his old self, the one she had fallen in love with and was beginning to see again, were a mirage. Max once again had chosen work over everything and everyone else. Devastated, she began to weep. This was the end of their relationship forever. Ray let her cry uninterrupted before he wheeled his chair over to talk it out. Abigail recounted seeing Max kiss Martha again and the subsequent fit she and her sisters had thrown, which had prompted Sally to make them go serve at the shelter, leaving their phones behind. Ray said he didn't know about the second kiss, but he had seen Jonah and Martha off and on all morning, attached at the hip, apparently well on their way to their new relationship. Abigail sat there even more dazed and confused.

Max's decision to accept the Paris gig had been a concession more than a decision, but he did love to travel, and he did love new challenges, so despite his broken heart, he did have some excited anticipation about this move. If Abigail were going to keep him at bay for another month or two, he wanted to be as far away as possible from her. He had left the mission without saying good-bye to anybody except Ray. He wasn't proud of that cowardly approach, but he didn't think he could face Aunt Sally or the Richards girls, especially Abigail. He would have seen the look of disdain and disappointment in her eyes and couldn't bear to have that memory while he was alone in a foreign country. And he didn't want to face

Jonah, either. Jonah would have accepted the rejection of his offer,

but he'd have found it inexcusable not to have told Abigail how

much he loved her before he left. The more he thought about how

he had left, the more ashamed he was. And why had Abigail blown

off their meeting? That was so unlike her. That dancefloor kiss

must have been too much to overcome, but didn't she know Max

hadn't initiated it? Max had tried to call her several times before he

left and eventually just left some general texts. Before he boarded

the plane, Max texted Abigail one more time. Maybe she would

finally respond. All he could think of to say was, "I'm sorry and I'll

miss you." He would reach out to Jonah and his brothers when he

arrived back in Chicago. He only had a couple of hours at home to

repack for at least three months abroad. Max sent one last text to

Renaldo, asking him to get some of his stuff out of storage to have

ready in his room.

Abigail couldn't help herself. As all the news settled into

her heart, she gasped and grabbed her mouth in horror. She started

to talk out loud to no one in particular, even though Ray was still in the room. "Max left Cocoa Beach and is leaving the country! Martha and Jonah are apparently starting a relationship. Ray and Sally are retiring from the mission. And, we still have a ton to do to get ready for an enormously important Valentine's Day Celebration because the mission is in financial ruin!" When she calmed back down, Ray explained to her further that Max had left in a rush once Abigail decided not to talk with him this morning. He was broken hearted, and Ray said he was pretty sure Max had intended to ask Abigail for another chance with their relationship. Now Abigail was really upset. Mad at Max and still confused by what she had seen, she still didn't want to lose the chance at forgiveness and redemption of their relationship. Every time she was faced with the truth about her response to Max's movements, her soulmate status with him was revealed. When Abigail pressed Ray again for this thoughts about Max's kissing Martha the second time, Ray acknowledged it was odd because Max had talked about only Abigail when they were in the office waiting for her. This confirmed again Abigail was not anywhere close to giving up on Max, but was he now giving up on her? And what in the world was going on with him and Martha?

Chapter 15

She started to cry again, so Ray encouraged her to run over and get her phone, check her messages, try and call Max, and talk to Sally and her sisters. Abigail knew all the girls were gone, but she heeded his advice and left the mission to head back to the house and be alone. There was no way she could work on the finances at that moment.

Deciding not to sulk in her room, Abigail instead grabbed her phone, saw the "I'm sorry, I'll miss you text," and was further confused. She tried to call Max, but his phone was obviously turned off, so she went to the kitchen, got an iced tea, and headed to the veranda. It was a beautiful day, she was still on vacation, and she could survive this new set back. She would figure the mess out with Max later. Besides, she really did want to consider moving to Florida to work at the mission, no matter who ended up the executive director. Accounting and business with purpose and service to help the community were what she had always wanted in her career. Moreover, she was going to try to convince Stephanie to come with her if she did take the job; there was enough work for two accountants for sure. Grateful Sally and Ray had given her the chance to consider it, she thought maybe she would move down to Cocoa sooner than later – get a fresh start, get away from the Chicago winter. But wow, she would really miss her family. She sat down, enjoying the breeze and the ocean, until her phone started buzzing repeatedly. Nine missed calls and three voice mails all loaded at once. She listened to the voice mails from Max, amazed at his openness and vulnerability. He expressed his love for her again – but also his confusion about whether or not Abigail even wanted him back – his last voice mail explaining why he had taken the job. For about the fifth time in 12 hours, Abigail bawled again.

When she gained composure, she called Stephanie to walk her through the latest drama. She had been on the phone with her for maybe 30 minutes when Martha and Jonah appeared in the distance, hand in hand, strolling slowly off the beach and toward the house. Abigail stared at them the whole time, becoming more indignant the closer they came. Ray was right. Martha was obviously making her move on Jonah, as well. Did she have no shame? The same day as kissing Max she strolled hand in hand with one of Max's best friends? And Jonah was falling for it? Abigail had started to like Martha, but this was taking it too far. She was going to confront

her as soon as she got within shouting distance. She told Stephanie

she had to go and would call her back later. She had to give Martha

a piece of her mind. Stephanie started to caution her friend from

that move, but Abigail ended the call before Stephanie could finish

her concern.

Chapter 16

Jonah and Martha meandered up to the veranda, now shoulder to shoulder, looking very much in love and making Abigail furious. In a fashion very uncharacteristic for her, she confronted both of them when they were still ten yards away. Her first verbal missile accused Martha of fooling around with two guys at the same time. Next, she accosted Jonah for bad judgment and backhanded friendship. Finally, she informed Jonah of the kiss Max and Martha had engaged in – just a few hours ago – that very morning. Instead of being defensive or argumentative, both Jonah and Martha had compassionate looks on their faces, making Abigail even madder. Even though Jonah and Martha were now on the veranda with her, she had been at full voice, and even as she calmed down and talked in a more reasonable volume, she maintained her terse tone. They still seemed unfazed by her accusations as she continued with questions, now concerning their response. Why did they both look at her so lovingly? Why wasn't Martha embarrassed or guilt-ridden? Why wasn't Jonah appalled at the woman, whom he still cuddled, even after her scarlet letter had been revealed?

When Abigail was done lashing out at them, Jonah asked if she were finished, and Abigail said yes. Looking to Martha for non-verbal approval, which he received with a nod of her head, Jonah, with his usual confidence and assurance, asked Abigail to sit down, prompting all three to gather around the table. Abigail was glad Jonah was speaking because she definitely did not want to hear Martha's rationalization for her two-timing ways and couldn't even look at her at the moment. Even though Abigail had directed most of the attack toward Martha, Jonah took the lead and explained both kiss events. He started with the dancefloor kiss. He assured Abigail, Martha agreeing via passionate head nods, it had nothing to do with Max, other than he was the kiss receiver. When Abigail noted Max did not seem to mind the kiss, Jonah burst into laughter and challenged Abigail to find a man in the country who wouldn't enjoy receiving a surprise kiss from Martha. Jonah's huge smile did make Abigail pause for a moment, and she admitted, internally at least, that no man in the state of Florida would have been repulsed by the unsolicited smooch. But still, Max didn't pull away. He let it linger. She had seen it with her own two eyes.

Chapter 16

Abigail moved on from the first kiss, still protesting the one from that morning she saw from her vista. Jonah again laughed and asked if she were talking about the kiss Max gave Martha or the kiss Max gave him? Abigail didn't understand, but Jonah's communication style, and his spirit of freedom and trust, started to turn her righteous anger into unsure confusion. Jonah explained Max ran into both of them on his way to meet Abigail, when Max had been on the way to the mission and they had been heading to the beach. Describing his rekindled passion for both life in general and Abigail in particular, Max Had been so glad and relieved he spontaneously hugged them both, told them he loved them, and kissed both of them on the cheek. The spontaneous kisses – borne of joy, not romance, invitation, or desire – celebrated the happy truth that one of his best friends and the woman who had incidentally placed herself between Max and his return to Abigail were now involved in the beginning of a relationship. More importantly, Max was 100% sure he wanted to marry Abigail, and soon. Furthermore, Jonah continued, Max had told Jonah all about Martha yesterday in

Daytona. He was trying to set Martha and Jonah up together. It was a part of Max's master plan for the week.

Abigail still wasn't completely sold on the notion and told Jonah she hadn't see him there this morning. All she had seen were Max and Martha. Jonah told her that was probably because after Max kissed him first, he had started laughing and backed down the alley towards the beach access entrance, which, he was willing to bet, was out of view from her window. They all looked at each other, and then Jonah and Martha followed Abigail, who had already burst upstairs to get a visual confirmation of this explanation.

Jonah was right. Abigail's view was obstructed from the northwest corner of the mission and from the alley to the beach access. Abigail was both thrilled and terrified by this admission. Her accidental observation of a friendship kiss had caused a cavalcade of responses that had now resulted in Max leaving for Paris! Abigail burst into tears yet again and collapsed on the bed. She apologized for accosting them and accusing them of betrayal and worse. Jonah and Martha forgave her immediately and told her so. But now, Abigail said, between sobs, the whole week and maybe her relationship with Max was ruined. Abigail told Jonah and Martha about Max's decision to leave for Paris because he thought he and Abigail were over, and now it was Jonah who was not happy with Max. Jonah suggested they drive to Orlando to catch him, but Abigail looked at her phone, saw it was ten minutes till his take off, and said not to bother calling; Max already had his phone turned off. Jonah tried anyway, to no avail. Well, at the very least, Abigail told them, she could text Max and finally let him know how she really felt. It had taken some random and chaotic experiences to help her recognize that again, but she was surer than ever that Max was the man for her. Even if he didn't change back completely, she was willing to love him wherever he was going, and for who he was right now. The rest could come later and when they were together, said Abigail, following up by thanking Jonah and Martha for their honesty and confession. After writing Max a heartfelt text, she resigned herself to waiting until Max arrived in Chicago to try and talk to him before he went overseas. Jonah said he had a much better idea, but they would have to talk to Ray and Sally about it first.

Chapter 17

Max had another window seat and another sad and dejected flight. For a couple of days, he had felt like his old self, even without the restoration of his relationship with Abigail. Until the Martha debacle, he had planned to tell Abigail he was sorry, he loved her, and he wanted another chance to marry her. Furthermore, he would marry her any day and any time she wanted. But, he had blown it once again. Even if the kiss was Martha's move, he still had spent a lot of time with her, and he could see why Abigail thought there might have been something to it. He got his phone out, but then decided to keep it off to try and forget about everything for a while. He would call his brothers and Jonah when he got to Chicago. He would stop to say good-bye to his parents on the way to his condo to pack all of his things. Fred was sending somebody to pick him up in the company limousine, so they would just have to make a few unexpected stops. He tried to get excited about the promotion and the opportunity to work in France, but he couldn't totally own it. It felt wrong. It felt as if he were running away. He napped briefly and woke up to hear they were about an hour away from the descent.

Max dreaded calling everybody to tell them the bad news when they landed. Wasn't that a sign, if you dread telling your family and friends about the biggest career move and promotion of your life? Didn't that indicate his concession was in fact a bad decision! What had he told Reginald and Felipe, that love was the most important thing? The only love involved in going to Paris was the love of self, love of status, love of money, and love of pleasing Fred and his colleagues. He hadn't mentioned any of those while sharing his deepest desires with Reginald and Felipe. Right then and there, Max realized he was making a big mistake.

Mike and Matt had to admit, even though they were tired from the long drive, they were excited to be in Florida, to be at the mission, and to hang out with Uncle Ray and Aunt Sally. They had made the trip in 16 hours and were in time for one of Aunt Sally's festive lunches, but when they arrived, everybody was in an uproar. Aunt Sally was in the kitchen cooking homemade pizzas, but Missy, Phoebe, Ray, Reginald, and Felipe were in the living room deep in conversation and concern. The girls all apologized and then gave the McGovern band members big hugs and welcomes. The two

Chapter 17

non-McGoverns were given the traditional Ray and Sally welcome and plates full of pizza and fries. The girls told the band to join them in the living room to hear the drama. Hardly any work on the celebration had been done today because Max and Abigail had had a big misunderstanding, culminating in Max's accepting a job in Paris for his firm and taking off for Chicago without saying goodbye to anybody except Ray. Abigail had thought Martha and Max had started a relationship when really it had been Jonah and Martha. And Max had two other job opportunities, one from Jonah in Daytona and one from Ray at the mission. Jonah, Martha, and Abigail had left as well. They had driven down to Daytona about two hours ago. They were taking Jonah's private jet to Chicago to catch Max before he flew across the ocean and made a huge mistake. Mike and Matt marveled at what they had missed, while their bandmates wondered aloud if this were always how the McGoverns and Richardses handled their vacations. Everybody answered with a resounding "Yes!"

Jonah had borrowed Ray's VW, which was certainly racking up some miles over the week, and sped down to Daytona Beach

Municipal Airport. He had called ahead so his plane was ready and fueled for them. Martha thought this was the coolest thing ever, falling more in love with Jonah by the minute. Abigail was excited, but nervous. This was not a move she would normally make, and she still wasn't 100% sure Max wanted to commit to marriage soon. As much as Abigail wanted to be married, she didn't want Max to marry her simply because he was afraid to lose her. That was not the right motivation for a romantic and true-love marriage. She wanted a proposal out of passionate love and out of a desire to be together forever, regardless of where that took them or if they were even apart once in a while. Jonah could tell Abigail was lost in her own thoughts and told her to snap out of it. He continued to challenge her to be prepared to simply tell her man what she wanted, why she wanted it, and what she planned to do about it. He told her to take charge. Her leadership would challenge and push Max to lead as he was supposed to, as he used to, and as he could again. He told her to quit the worry, forget about the hurt feelings, and release her own heart. Jonah should be a counselor like her mom, Abigail thought to herself. That thought made her instantly call her parents

164

and talk to them about everything that had happened. She walked them through the ordeal as quickly as she could, asking them to call Max's parents to let them know what was happening. Jonah and Martha gave Abigail noise privacy in the back seat and drove in silence, but they held hands the entire ride. When they arrived at the airport, Jonah showed his identification, which allowed him to drive the old van right to the hangar where the plane was waiting. Abigail hung up when they parked, boarded the plane, then put her phone away when the pilot asked them to turn off their phones for a while.

The Marauders were exhausted from the long travel, so Mike asked Sally if they could get themselves unpacked and settled in for the day, after which they would come downstairs for dinner. They pledged to work their tails off tomorrow, but they needed to have an easy night. Sally assured them this was a wise and appropriate agenda and asked the men to follow her upstairs, where she had their room ready. As was the case for at least half of their road shows, the band would have to share a room, so it didn't bother them a bit. Right before Matt started up the second tier of stairs, Missy asked him if he wanted to head down to Daytona with her to pick up some more items for the silent auction, which business friends of Jonah's had dropped off at JW Inc. How Jonah arranged so many things on the side was impressive. He was constantly texting and emailing on his phone while he engaged with anyone, multi-tasking significant decisions and communications while never being distant or disengaged. Since Matt had done the bulk of the driving from Chicago and was exhausted, he told Missy as long as she drove, he would love to go with her and catch-up. Looking for approval, Matt eyed Mike, who, along with the others, gave Matt a hard time about passing up sleep for a woman. It didn't matter to them Missy, who blushed and turned away, was standing right there. Matt did not confirm or deny their accusations, giving them all a big smile and raised eyebrows as he bounded down the stairs to join Missy. Fatigue can be erased easily for the chase of love.

The plane landed uneventfully, with Max more convinced than ever he was making a mistake – but how to get out of his predicament? He pulled out his phone, turned it on, and grimaced as he noticed he had forgotten to charge it during his hasty exit from Cocoa, leaving him only a 2% battery life remaining. He saw he had seven missed calls, three from Abigail, three from Jonah, and one

from Fred. He also started to read what seemed like a frantic text

from Abigail when his phone died, which elicited a guttural noise of

frustration. As was his practice, he was one of the last ones off the

plane. He always wondered what the rush was when you had to go

to baggage claim and wait more anyway. Strolling casually into the

terminal, Max was startled to see Fred waiting for him. Fred asked

if Max had received his voice mail about a change in plans. Max

informed him of his dead phone and asked what the change was.

Fred said that there was a connecting flight to Paris in an hour, so

they had to grab that flight today. They had a dinner meeting with

the executive team from Carpentier tomorrow night, and France was

seven hours ahead of their time. Fred had taken the liberty to work

with Ronaldo and had gone into Max's apartment to load another

suitcase full of his nicer clothes. Max was glad but also slightly

offended his boss had been roaming around in his condo. At least

he kept a clean and organized place. Max shrugged his shoulders

and told Fred that was fine. He hoped they would have time to eat

before they moved into the international terminal, but they didn't.

Max asked to borrow Fred's phone and left his parents a message about the change in plans. They didn't answer, which was odd, but he left a voice mail. That was the only call he had time to make.

Jonah, Martha, and Abigail made better time than the commercial jet and were on schedule to be at O'Hare in plenty of time to meet Max and to let Abigail confront him with her love. Unfortunately, O'Hare would not let Jonah's pilot land the plane at their airport. It was not uncommon for large airports to limit individual and corporate planes during their busiest times. When exactly did O'Hare *not* have busy times? Jonah thought. Midway Airport, Chicago's second airport, would also not let the plane land, so now they were left with DuPage Municipal Airport, which though not terribly inconvenient from the standpoint of the flight itself, would result in a 45-minute, minimum, automobile commute to O'Hare – assuming no bad traffic or incidents. They were going to be cutting it really close, but Abigail speculated out loud that if they missed Max at the airport, they could always go to his condo and catch him there. She called Mark and Maisy to see if they had heard anything about the time of Max's connecting flight, but they had not yet heard from Max. They told Abigail they loved her, and they hoped it worked out for the best. Abigail called Max, left another voice mail, and texted Max again, but still no response. Not even Jonah had a new plan that would avert this diversion. The landing at DuPage was a bit tumultuous as they came right into a head wind, a perfect metaphor for the ordeal of the day. As usual, there were a car and driver waiting for them. Jonah was as free and relaxed as always. Martha wanted Abigail and Max to get back together, but she was invested in the wild journey as much as she was the romantic fulfillment of her friends. Abigail was stressed out of her mind and wanted to throw up.

Fred and Max made it through customs in time to grab some Chinese food, eating it at a public table. Their plane departed in 15 minutes. Max, starved, devoured his food in impressive fashion. Shocked Fred was going to Paris with him, Max was nevertheless glad to have some company and not to have to be alone for a while. It also helped him to forget all the people to whom he still had to apologize for his sophomoric departure. He was much more comfortable asking for forgiveness than asking for permission.

He found it easier to explain himself after the fact than inform

somebody of his intention and risk a contrarian decision or direction

from what he intended to pursue – or worse, to hear their

disappointment in or disapproval of his course of action. He

realized this immaturity and lack of accountability, vowing to work

on it while in Paris. A few minutes after Max's trip to the airport

convenient store to buy a ridiculously priced charging chord, the

plane began to load. Unlike Max, Fred only flew first class, so they

had to board first. Max looked around the terminal before he

followed Fred down the gangway and onto the massive jet. He

didn't know who or what he was looking for, but he felt he probably

wouldn't be back in Chicago for a long time.

Sure enough, the traffic from DuPage to O'Hare was awful.

They weren't going to make it, so they decided to change plans.

Abigail called Stephanie and asked her if she would leave work early

to go down to Max's condo to see if she could catch him there.

Stephanie was thrilled to be a part of the great Max marriage caper

and said she wouldn't even tell Mary Anne. During the phone call,

Abigail realized Stephanie and Martha had similar personalities.

Chapter 17

They were always up for an adventure or an intervention. They didn't worry about their schedule or their plans. If somebody or something needed their attention, and it was a worthwhile alteration or adjustment, they just did it. Abigail vowed to work on that freedom as soon as this chaos was over. For now, she prayed their plan worked and tried to rest in the back seat of the limo.

Chapter 18

Max remembered to charge his phone once they were buckled into their first-class seats. Fred was super excited for the trip and talked more in the first hour of the flight than Max had heard him talk in years. During a break in the conversation, Max asked him if he thought Max's chutzpah and moxie were back? Fred stopped talking, turned and looked at Max, and said if it weren't, there was no way Max would have agreed to this spontaneous opportunity.

Max smiled and thanked him, but inside, he knew the chutzpah and moxie were back because he had been away from the corporate world, the corporate pressure, and the bottom-line, profit-making mindset, not because of this trip to Paris. He made a decision right there and at that exact moment. This Paris job was the last one he was going to do for Fred and the company. When this was over, he was moving to Florida and either working for Jonah or taking over for Ray at the mission. He would really love if he could do both, but either role was fifty hours a week, so that crazy dream wasn't worth the time. With that emphatic mental decision resolved, Max's mood and spirit completely lightened, he was able to relax more, and he sat back to enjoy the rest of the really long flight.

Stephanie ran into the lobby of Max's condo association and right into Ronaldo. Pausing for a moment to take in the handsome doorman, she then erupted in a five-minute stream of consciousness. She told Ronaldo she was Abigail's best friend and that she needed to find Max immediately because he was making a big mistake and needed to marry Abigail as soon as possible. Ronaldo smiled and laughed at Stephanie's passionate disclosure but then sadly informed her Max's boss had come earlier in the afternoon, packed Max a new suitcase, and headed to O'Hare. They were probably already in the air to France by now. Stephanie let out an audible "NO!" and then asked Ronaldo to help her find a place to sit down. As Ronaldo escorted her to a lounge, she grabbed her phone to call Abigail to tell her the awful news. After Ronaldo brought Stephanie a water bottle, he suggested she sit and relax for a while before jumping right back into traffic. He also told her that she was right – Max did need to marry Abigail soon – partly because Ronaldo was tired of beating Max so soundly at squash; Max had no game without Abigail in his life. "And," Ronaldo added, "I'm not just talking about squash." Stephanie was instantly smitten with Ronaldo and wanted to engage in more conversation, but Ronaldo had to excuse himself and go back to his station outside. He winked, smiled, and walked through the revolving door. Stephanie paused for a moment before remembering the urgency of her phone call she needed to make. She hit the recent-calls icon and touched her best friend's name.

Abigail ended the call with Stephanie and relayed the bad news to Jonah and Martha. Then she began to cry. She had cried more in the last two days than she had since she was a little girl. This is the reason she didn't do crazy, spur-of-the-moment things, she told Jonah and Martha. Her spontaneous efforts never worked out and left her frazzled, exhausted, and emotional. When she apologized for wasting their time and Jonah's money, he sternly told her to quit being a baby and asked her why this quest was now over. Even Martha was surprised by Jonah's lack of empathy and sensitivity to Abigail, giving an inquisitive look to her new boyfriend. Jonah was just getting started. He told Abigail that Max was her man. He had been since they were ten years old. Why would she give up on a seventeen-year relationship because a change of flight times altered their game plan? His stomach rumbling, Jonah suggested they go to Abigail's place, order some pizza, make a new game plan, and then get some sleep. They were all running on about four hours of sleep, and it was catching up with them. The more Abigail hung around Jonah, the more she realized why he was a multi-millionaire and why he was so successful at so many different ventures. Nothing deterred him from his focus and his vision. His clarity of mission and vision were remarkable, and the grown-up version of Jonah was even more appealing and compelling than the college version. The more Martha observed and engaged with Jonah, the more in love she fell. She had fallen quickly before, but this was ridiculous. She would marry him on the spot and had no doubts, fears, or worries about what kind of amazing life they would live. But why wasn't he married yet?

Chicago-to-Paris is about an eight-hour flight, and France is seven hours ahead of Chicago, so though their flight left around 6:00 p.m., Chicago time, on Wednesday, it would land at 9:00 a.m., France time, on Thursday. Fred stopped talking after two nonstop hours of business conversation, with which Max was bored after about 15 minutes. His work with Fred, and Fred himself, Max realized, actually wore him out. It was subtle, but he had to pretend he was something that he wasn't around Fred. He had to be zealous, intense, and passionate about things he actually wasn't zealous, intense, or passionate about. That in itself was a revelation. Even though he was talented at his marketing and sales role, it didn't mean he had to do it. There were other options for him in life and in career. It had been less than a week since his mandated vacation, but it had been one of the most important weeks of his life. He sighed deeply, tilted his seat back, draped himself in a blanket, and went fast to sleep.

Jonah had the driver stop at Jerry and Joan's house prior to terminating their day at Abigail's place. When Abigail had called her mother an hour ago to update her on all the new craziness, Joan had immediately invited them all over for dinner. Joan not only loved to cook but also to invite people into her home. She remembered Jonah had been over to their house a couple of times when they were all in college, and she also remembered Martha and was quite intrigued by the pairing Jonah declared was officially official – very loudly – while Abigail talked with her on the phone. Of course, the driver and Stephanie were also invited to come eat, no questions asked. Since Stephanie had returned to her and Abigail's apartment after striking out on her quest to catch Max at the condo, she was glad to come join Mrs. Richards and the family for a meal. They all had a great time at dinner, and once Jerry spilled the beans about both sets of parents flying down to Florida for the celebration and dance, Jonah insisted that the Richardses and the McGoverns cancel their flight and fly back with them on his private jet. Once Jonah made declarations of intent, there was really no argument or excuses he would accept, so after a few mild protests, the Richardses and McGoverns received the blessing. Jonah also invited Stephanie to come with them for the weekend, to which she, without hesitation, responded with an enthusiastic "yes." She had days saved up, but she didn't really care if she were fired. When they speculated about a return flight home, Jonah said he would be honored to provide that, as well. Besides, he said, he needed to spend some more time in Chicago soon, leaning over and giving Martha a passionate kiss right in front of everybody.

Chapter 19

Thursday

Mike and Matt stepped right into the holes left by Martha, Max, and Jonah, working with Sally and Missy to finalize all the silent-auction items and preparing the starting-bid documentation. They also tore down the tables and chairs in the community room at the mission to prepare for the dance. Half of the Valentine's Day event was outside and half was inside. That way they were always prepared in case of bad weather, and it also diversified the congestion, allowing people to come in and out of the mission. That is where the environment and family spirit of the mission was shown best. The two other bandmates and Phoebe focused on that. They spent the whole morning cleaning, organizing, and displaying the history, the work, the adventures, and the success stories of the mission. Phoebe also decided to make a tribute board for Ray and Sally. Even though they had not announced their retirement publicly yet, she wanted to make sure they were honored while they were still running the mission.

The game plan that Jonah, Martha, and Abigail decided upon was simple, but fun and playful, as well. After she and Stephanie returned to their apartment, Abigail left a series of 14 voice mails for Max, a series of accumulating stories and disclosures of how much she loved him and why she wanted to be his wife. She also spoke about freedom for the first time in their relationship. Her first voice mail said she forgave Max for the Martha incident, but more importantly, she forgave him for getting lazy and complacent in their relationship. Stephanie edited, monitored, and held Abigail accountable for every voice mail message. Abigail wrote them out first, with Stephanie helping her be more assertive and directly honest with edits of her content. Abigail said she wanted to marry Max soon and didn't want to get married on their college graduation date anymore. That date now had negative connotations. She wanted to get married whenever Max wanted, and she was willing to wait – no matter how long. Her last voice mail said she was going to accept the job offer at the mission and move to Florida by March. She told Max she didn't care if Max stayed with VanStevens, worked for Jonah, or worked for the mission; they could figure out how to navigate a long-distance relationship and make it work. She was

tired of letting other things and other people get in the way of their

forever love. When she was done with the last voice mail, Abigail

celebrated with Stephanie. Uninhibited, she danced around her

apartment, and Stephanie would not let her dance alone.

Fred and Max toured Paris on their way to the villa Fred

had rented in Montmartre, a part of the Right Bank in the art district.

The villa was amazing, filled with antiques and famous paintings but

still with modern amenities. Fred and Max, both exhausted from

the flight and the jet lag, had a 3 p.m. early dinner with their client's

executive team, so it would have to be a quick nap. Max finally had

time to catch-up with his phone and saw he had over 20 messages

from Abigail. He really wanted to sleep, but he couldn't stand the

anticipation of knowing what Abigail found so important she had to

leave 20 messages, which was so unlike Abigail – so unrestrained, so

impulsive. Giving up his nap time, he lay down on his bed and

listened to 30 minutes of confession, self-disclosure, and freedom

messages from the woman he loved. He was blown away with her

honesty, her vulnerability, her new spirit. By the time he had listened to the third voice mail, he was as restrained as he could be, pacing around the villa, smiling from ear to ear, crying and laughing at the same time. As soon as he finished all 14, he wanted to call her immediately, but Fred yelled across the hallway that the driver would be there in 10 minutes and Max had to shower, shave, and get ready in a hurry. He called her quickly, only reaching her voice mail. How fitting, he thought. He left her a very quick message, professing his love for her, thanking her for the forgiveness, the open and honest disclosures, and the free spirit for the future. He had also been thinking a lot about his life and his future and wanted to talk to her as soon as he could. He ended the call, stripped down as fast as he could, and jumped into the shower.

The executive dinner and meeting went fantastically. The food was incredible, the wine was exquisite, and the pastries for dessert were the best Max had ever tasted. He so wished Abigail could have been there with him to experience it. He promised himself to bring Abigail back to Paris for their honeymoon, whenever that was. The business conversation after the dinner, even with the language barriers, also went extremely well. Fred had never seen Max that alive, that connected and focused. This was the Max

he had hired and believed in enough to promote him to director

more quickly than anybody else in his company. Fred was also in

his element, reminiscing with the CEO of Carpentier about their

humble beginnings and the way they had forged forward despite

great risk and unproven alliances. Max really enjoyed seeing that

side of Fred and told him so when they were in the car on the way

home. Fred returned the favor, expressing his appreciation for

Max's people skills and instinct for informal relational negotiations.

Fred told Max he had just witnessed an even higher level of chutzpah

and moxie than he anticipated. He said whatever happened in

Florida for those five days must have been special. Max said that it

was – it was really special, and he actually learned some significant

truths about himself he had been avoiding for some time now. Fred

was curious and asked Max to elaborate. Max, fully embracing his

new truth-telling spirit, decided to follow his convictions and gave

Fred a recap of the craziness of the past five days, culminating in the

trip to France. Fred, enthralled by the narrative, didn't interrupt

once, not the normative conversation pattern for the demanding

CEO. Max took advantage of the spirit they shared and informed Fred that, in light of all he had learned about himself, this was going to be his last assignment for VanStevens. Furthermore, he needed to leave tomorrow to return to Florida and would be back on Sunday night. Fred could tell that Max had already made up his mind, so he didn't bother to counter and wasn't visibly upset. "It's about time," Fred added, as a punctuation to the declaration his young protégé had just made. Max stared out the car window and realized he finally knew what Ray had meant with his cryptic texts.

Jonah and Martha spent the rest of Thursday touring Northwestern, Martha's home and neighborhood, and various sights in Chicago. With those two souls together, there would not be a dull or boring moment for as long as their relationships lasted. Abigail was also now at the place where she really hoped Jonah and Martha would get married and find forever love together. How fast her opinion and heart had changed about the two people whom she thought had betrayed her just 24 hours earlier. If this was living life in the present and without fear or over planning, she was starting to like it. She was enjoying a more relaxed day, doing laundry, baking cookies, and watching her Netflix show. Stephanie came over around 6 p.m., told Abigail it had been a terrible day at work, and mentioned Mary Anne had asked about her several times. Stephanie did not reveal to Mary Anne Abigail was in town, but Mary Anne had seen a post about their adventure on Instagram. Abigail told Stephanie informing Mary Anne she was leaving Anderson, leaving Chicago, and going to Florida would not be easy, but she was prepared to do it and probably should do it soon. Jonah and Martha came back home around 9:00 and, if possible, they looked more in love than when they had left that morning. Jonah said he might have to buy a business up here; he had forgotten how much he loved Chicago. None of the ladies doubted his sincerity and wondered how long it would be before that became a reality.

When Max finally returned to his room, he found a wrapped gift for him on his bed. It was from Jonah. Who else would be able to track him down that fast and orchestrate a cross-country delivery within a few hours? In the box was a beautiful picture frame, but without a picture in it. In an envelope was a sealed card with Max's name on it. It was a note from Jonah saying, "It's your life. Your portrait. Your future. Who is in the picture with you?" As usual, his friend had challenged Max's heart right when he needed the push and accountability to follow through on his new life decisions. Finally, he picked up his phone, scrolled the messages from Abigail, listened to the last one again, and called her. They laughed, cried, teased, encouraged, and challenged each other for an hour before Max had to leave for one last commitment with Fred before he flew back. Max had found a flight that would get him to Florida by 8:00 Friday night. It wasn't ideal, and it would be awful flying back and forth across the ocean, but for Abigail and the Heart and Soul Rescue Mission, it was worth it. He also made up his mind he was declaring his love for Abigail in front of everybody at the Valentine's Day dance. He had always shied away from any kind of public presentation of their relationship, and he now realized that in doing so, he had never honored or socially declared how special Abigail was to him. That was going to change now. That was going to change in a big way.

Chapter 20

Friday

Max decided not to tell Abigail he was coming back to Florida for the celebration. He had to leave the villa at 5:00 in the morning, so he called for a taxi rather than having the company driver take him to the airport. He had called Abigail around 4:00 a.m., France time, and 10:00 p.m., Chicago time, to have a 20-minute conversation before she went to bed. Abigail told Max Jonah was flying them all back to Florida – the rest of both of their families and the hot and heavy dynamic duo of Jonah and Martha. The call was like their phone conversations from college, more about their friendship than about decisions, business, or schedules. Abigail told Max about their crazy day trying to catch him, and they both agreed it had worked out better for Max to reach the decision about VanStevens on his own before he even listened to Abigail's voice mails. They talked about dreams and about their future together. The last topic they covered was which Florida job Max was going to take. They talked about the pros and cons of each, acknowledging it was a really hard decision. Max said he wanted to talk to both Jonah and Ray one more time before he made up his mind, but either way, he was moving to Florida by the summer and would join Abigail in the Cocoa Beach and Daytona region. Max asked Abigail not to talk to either of them before he did – he would try to do so before the end of the day – so it wouldn't be too weird for her when everybody asked her how the Max chase went.

This time when Max sat by his window seat in the airplane, he was happy, upbeat, and ready to work on his laptop. He had some huge visions and movements stirring in his soul, with an eight-hour flight to craft his dream for Florida. The last thing Max did before he left Paris, while on the way to the airport, was call his and Abigail's parents. He apologized to them for his indecision, his lack of leadership, and his questionable character the last several years. He told them that he was ending his work with VanStevens after this Paris job and moving to Florida to join Abigail forever. Both sets of parents were extremely happy for him and for Abigail. They told him they were sad he would not be able to join the rest of the family at the Valentine's Day Celebration. They also bragged about their upcoming flight to Florida in Jonah's plane. Max said they would need to plan a trip every year together now that he and Abigail would be in Florida. They all agreed this was an excellent idea; maybe they would rotate which season they came to Cocoa Beach based on different holidays or special events for the mission. Just like the old days, they would mix some serving and purpose to the vacations.

Jonah and Martha were up at dawn and went out for a morning run. Abigail and Stephanie ate breakfast in their pajamas and finished packing. Jonah had thought ahead, and his driver had already exchanged their car for a big airport shuttle van. They picked up both sets of parents and their luggage, reaching the DuPage Airport around 10:30, in the air by 11. They would get to Daytona airport around 3:30. Abigail, Jonah, and Martha told the epic story of the relational gymnastics that had taken place over the past five days, entertaining the families for half the flight. There was a lot to tell. Joan had a story to add, announcing Missy and Matt were hitting it off again, and Sally relayed they had stayed up half the night talking in the living room. Everyone agreed there was something special about Ray and Sally's place and the Heart and Soul Rescue Mission. Love seemed to live and grow there.

Ray and Sally had never had a wilder week of preparation and chaos before a big event like this one. There had been ten different people helping and eight people living with them; normally one person helped, and no one housed with them. It led to some very hectic and challenging organization, but Sally was an excellent people mover and felt they should be finished with everything they needed to do by the early afternoon. Ray just hoped this wasn't the last Valentine's Day Celebration. He knew the silent auction would not cover the full amount of the debt they owed, so they needed some new investors or more sponsors like Big Beef Steakhouse to keep the mission open. Sally had the day's assignments and a hot breakfast on the kitchen island, but the remaining ladies went to serve at the women's shelter before the Marauders even awoke. Matt and Mike had forgotten how much fun and how much hard work went into a trip to the Heart and Soul Rescue Mission. Their main assignment of the day was setting up all their equipment – the lights, the sound, the floor monitors – and running a sound check.

That was in their regular pre-show day, but they all expressed interest in finishing before lunch, so they could help everyone else in the afternoon.

The JW Express touched down peacefully in Daytona ahead of schedule, just as Jonah liked it. Sally had told them through a group text there was no more work to do for the celebration, so they could enjoy a quick tour of JW's facilities if they wished. That always motivated Jonah, who loved to show the innovative technology his company used in the sports and recreation field. His driver had called another employee, so another van was waiting for them, and after a quick dinner at the closest diner, the JW tour began. He even showed them his Northwestern basketball court, something he rarely showed anyone who was not an employee of the company. Abigail told Jonah he had to let the Heart and Soul Saturday basketball guys play there sometime. It would be the coolest basketball experience most of them would ever have. Jonah loved the idea and promised to talk to Ray about it sometime that night or tomorrow.

After working on his new business plan, Max was able to sleep for a good chunk of his flight. He couldn't wait to see Abigail and finally walk along the beach with her, but he also was really excited to show Ray and Jonah what he had created as a potential business plan. He rented a car at the airport and was on the road toward Cocoa Beach a little before 9 p.m. He speculated he would be back at Ray and Sally's a little after 10:00 p.m. He gave a call to his contact at Big Beef Steakhouse to make sure they had the delivery time accurate for the banquet and thanked them once again for their donations and sponsorship. Max assured them he would be the one handling this account now and would reciprocate the good will and market their new restaurant in Cocoa Beach as soon as it opened. He did this without assurance of his business plan moving forward but with assurance of his own word and commitment to the area and the mission.

Jonah's van pulled into Ray and Sally's around 8:30 p.m. Mark, Maisy, Jerry, and Joan still had to go to their hotel, but they wanted to say hello to everyone first. The group of eight poured through the front door, precipitating another round of reunion and tears. Matt and Mike played their guitars on the veranda, creating a festive atmosphere inside the house and out. Missy and Phoebe sat outside enjoying the ocean breeze. The other two band members, perched on the disclosure couch, were under the spell of Ray and Sally's questions. Stephanie stopped to stare at the two handsome men before Abigail moved her attention elsewhere. Once again Martha was moved by this display of love and affection and told Jonah that she hoped her family would be like that one day. Jonah assured her this would be the case and then motioned for Martha, Abigail, and Stephanie to follow him through the sea of family and out onto the veranda, where the music and wine flowed.

Max had to park at the mission because there were no spaces near Ray and Sally's. He had terrible jet lag but couldn't have cared less. He was so excited to surprise everybody and so glad to be there for the celebration. The spontaneity had cost him about $1,000, but he wasn't concerned with that cost. He was back to following his heart and his convictions, no matter what the sacrifice. It felt great. He felt great. He heard the music playing from the side of the house and followed his brothers' rhythms until he lingered behind the beach side of the veranda. Once the song reached the chorus again, he appeared from the shadows, headed toward the stairs, and sang the third part of the harmony before they could even see him. Abigail was the first to see his face, and uninhibited, ran towards him and jumped into his arms. Max twirled her around while he told her how much he loved her. His brothers looked at each other and both instinctively switched to playing the song that Max had written for Abigail when the band first formed, "Forever Love." Max asked Abigail if she would dance with him, and they strolled to the deck floor hand in hand, where Jonah and Martha joined them. Eventually so did Ray and Sally, Mark and Maisy, and Jerry and Joan, who had heard the commotion and the shouts of Max's name. After the song ended, Max made the rounds hugging everyone and shared his frantic past 48 hours. Finally, everyone returned to regular conversation and eating, but it was getting close to midnight. Abigail had been by Max's side the whole time he talked and connected with both families, but finally he turned to Abigail and asked her to walk with him along the beach for 30 minutes before they went to bed. Everybody watched them wander down to the beach, everyone sporting huge smiles of relief and joy.

Max shared with Abigail his vision for their Florida venture together – with passion, tears, excitement, and childlike faith. The vision included Heart and Soul and JW Enterprises. Abigail absolutely loved it and couldn't wait for Max to share it with Ray and Jonah. When they arrived back at the house, no one was around, and the house was totally quiet. They assumed the party must have ended shortly after they left, everyone recognizing the huge day in front of them. Max texted both Ray and Jonah to meet him tomorrow morning at 7 at the Pink Flamingo Diner. He wanted Reginald and Felipe to hear his vision also. Ray didn't answer, but he awoke early every day and wouldn't miss the request. Jonah responded with a thumbs up emoji and a picture of him and Martha at a club dancing. Max and Abigail just shook their heads in amazement.

At the burn pit in the sand, halfway between the ocean and the veranda, Max asked Abigail what she envisioned for her role as administrator at the mission until their master plan could be implemented. She happily shared all the changes she wanted and needed to make in order to get the finances back in good stead. It would not be as difficult as Ray feared, as long as Max could land a few more sponsors and they could streamline some services the mission used. She also had multiple ways she believed she could generate new revenue from the services the mission provided to the community, without creating undue expenses for the people. When they were about to return to the house, Max stopped Abigail, turned her to face him, and bent down on one knee in the sand. He pulled out the engagement ring Abigail had returned to him three months ago and asked her to marry him once again. Abigail shouted out a "yes," and the couple embraced, held each other, and stared out at the ocean and the future now before them.

Chapter 21

Saturday

Max and Abigail woke up early enough to see Martha and Jonah head to the beach for their morning workout, though they had probably slept for about four hours. It seemed the happy couple had been together for years. Max looked at his watch, worrying that Jonah wouldn't make it to the diner, but then laughed out loud at himself. He didn't need to monitor or keep Jonah accountable to anything. He would be there, Max thought, as he and Abigail started their walk to the diner, whose party room in the back Max had called ahead to reserve. Max wasn't nervous at all; if anything, he was a little too amped up and worried he would overwhelm Ray with his ideas. He knew there was nothing he could say, present, or project that would overwhelm Jonah, who had already heard some of the possibilities. Jonah would love the fact Max had run with them and fleshed them out fuller without him. In fact, he was more worried about underwhelming Jonah, knowing his friend had probably already thought about a ton of creative strategies to save the mission, invest further in the community, and expand the JW brand all at the same time. It was just four days ago, Max thought, that he had walked this same path, wondering what had happened to his life. Now he was arm and arm with his bride-to-be, about ready to introduce their new career and ministry. They passed right around the corner where Abigail had seen the second Martha and Max kiss. She paused, grabbed his arm, showed Max the window angle, reminding him how it had happened, and planted a deep kiss on Max to make up for her inaccurate interpretation of said event.

The celebration started at 9 a.m., so everyone else was also up early, enjoying a huge breakfast spread Sally, Joan, and Maisy had prepared for them before they left for the women's shelter. Their assignments for the day had been finalized by Missy and Sally the night before and left out on the island, so there wouldn't be any surprises. Matt and Missy had driven their parents to their hotel Friday night, taking the opportunity to inform them of their decision to date again. They didn't ask their permission, but in light of everything else going on in the family, they figured it would be better to tell them up front.

Jonah made it to the restaurant on time, Martha in tow. They didn't go anywhere without each other right now. Ray came by himself. Max invited Reginald and Felipe to join them, and though they were thrilled by the invitation, they were a tad hesitant to leave their table, so it took them a while to gather their things for the move across the restaurant. Everyone helped the two old timers and gave them seats that were easy to get to in the meeting room. The room was set up in a big U, with everyone seated and facing Max, who now stood at the front of the room. Ray took the first chair to the right, both nervous and excited about this presentation. He believed he had seen the real Max come back over the last week and hoped he was back for good. He would find out in a few minutes.

Max took a huge drink of water and then proceeded to lay out his plan, a masterful combination of entrepreneurial spirit, partnership with a new corporate entity, and franchising/expansion. Heart and Soul Rescue Mission would become a non-profit 503C under the JW Inc. umbrella, which would create a new division in the non-profit sector. This new arm would be called Cast the Net.

Max made sure to catch eyes with Abigail when he announced the name, and she beamed. He had told her about the umbrella under JW, but he had not told her the name. JW Inc. would absorb the debt in the takeover and also purchase two more properties in Daytona for the first of five more Heart and Soul Rescue Missions along the Atlantic Coast, a plan Jonah and Max had hatched on Monday night while they drove around Daytona – the very idea Max had gone to Daytona to discuss with Jonah in the first place. He hadn't gone there for a donation for Heart and Soul; he had wanted Jonah to buy out Heart and Soul. Jonah had loved the idea and had already been running numbers and figures with his guys, so he interrupted Max's presentation to pull up a PowerPoint showing the five locations his team had already located for future Heart and Soul sites. He and Max had talked about two locations, and, of course, Jonah had expanded that idea. The moment Ray affirmed and signed the buy-out paperwork, offers on the properties would begin. There would also be a new Rescue Mission Basketball League for youth, with the championship to be played at the basement of the Northwestern gym. Max and Jonah would each coach a team and make sure to recruit other coaches. Jonah's leadership team had also spotted two different buildings in Daytona that would work for two new women's shelters. The name of these shelters would be Aunt Sally's. Martha chimed in that one of Jonah's executives had already made progress with the city for purchase, zoning, and renovation plans.

Max resumed the presentation, detailing how Jonah would become the owner of the Heart and Soul Rescue Mission brand, and they wanted Ray to be the chair of the new board he would create for Cast the Net. He promised Ray it would only meet three times per year. Max would become the CEO, with Abigail the CFO. Martha would become the JW Inc. interior designer, and Max and Jonah really hoped Missy would join the JW family and become Cast the Net's COO. They just hadn't had a chance to lay out the whole plan to her yet. Initially, Max and Abigail would both work out of Cocoa Beach, with Martha and Missy working out of Daytona. They would oversee the initial build outs of the two new facilities there and eventually the four other ones. Lastly, JW Enterprises was going to invest $500,000 into the Cocoa Beach Heart and Soul facility and an equal amount into the Aunt Sally's Women's Shelters, at which point Jonah piped in with the information that he had purchased the property yesterday. He planned to bring it under the Cast the Net umbrella, allowing him to partner the two entities together in every city.

Ray sat absolutely stunned, tears running down his cheeks. Reginald and Felipe had briskly risen out of their seats to give a standing ovation. Everyone else in the room erupted in joyful excitement and exuberance. Eventually the room quieted down again, and everyone looked at Ray. He still sat stoically, without moving or saying a thing, for at least another minute. Ray had expected some new ideas that would probably be innovative and, of course, some type of potential plan to save the mission. But this complete metamorphosis, with over a $1M of cash invested into Heart and Soul and the women's shelter was too much for his weathered heart and soul to handle. He finally stood up and walked around the room, crying openly now and without shame, and gave each one of them an enormous bear hug. Eventually, he sat back down and, after a few deep breaths, finally was able to say thank you.

He loved the plan, which was greater than anything he could have imagined. Lastly, as he choked back some more tears, he said his favorite part was the naming of the women's shelter after Sally. Before he finished, he asked for another huge favor. Could Max and Jonah roll out the new concept, name, and movements tonight at the banquet? He thought that, along with the new sponsorship from Big Beef, this kind of news would invigorate the Cocoa Beach city leaders in the mission and its future. Ray thought it would be worth several more donations from potential partners in attendance. Jonah, never one to worry about potential risks to an early announcement, told Ray of course he and Max would present it tonight. Max knew this meant Jonah would have to work the phone and maybe even visit a few leaders this afternoon, but once Jonah was locked in, he was locked in. He also knew Jonah would require Max to deliver it. Reginald and Felipe were smiling from ear to ear, mostly because they could tell Jonah and Martha and Max and Abigail were in love and going to do this together. Just before they left to finish their breakfast at their normal table, they asked if the men could somehow include their sons' business in some of the remodeling work. Jonah shouted an exuberant "Yes, of course."

Unfortunately, there was not much time to sit and reflect on the grand vision other than to celebrate it. Everyone hustled back to the house and changed into their celebration Heart and Soul shirts and headed for their stations of responsibility. Now that Max and Jonah were taking over as the faces of Cast the Net, Ray wanted them to work the crowd, so he could introduce them to all the key civic leaders of the community. Jonah also informed them he had invited many of the civic leaders from Daytona to come tonight, as well. At the house, the main floor was jam packed with all the family, everyone expressing sincere excitement for the day. Ray whistled to get everyone's attention and then asked Max to give a quick recap of the new movements prior to the celebration's starting. Following the five-minute explanation, the room erupted in applause and hugs, after which Ray asked everyone to hold hands as he offered a prayer of blessing. After the "amen," Missy said she was honored about her potential role but told Jonah she would be expensive. Jonah laughed and told her to name her salary, and no one in the room thought he was teasing. Missy promised to pray about it for sure, but she wanted to talk with Matt about it first, eliciting cheers from all in response to their obvious commitment. Raising her voice above the clamor, Sally spoke up and told the group to break up and get to their stations.

Big Beef Steakhouse delivered on time and in excess. The mission and the shelter would have several meals from the leftovers and be able to feed the whole community at the Sunday meal. The food was great, the decorations were fantastic, the atmosphere was electric, and the place was jammed. They had to set up some extra tables in the hallway, which was not ideal, but no one complained. Abigail made note that renovations for future celebrations should include a larger space for big meetings and texted Martha and Missy with her ideas and observations all day long. Everything went forward without a hitch, and the hours flew by as they served and shared with the community. Each volunteer was able to take two 30-minute breaks, but nobody did.

Finally, it was time for the banquet, the first time the McGovern and Richards families had sat down and rested. The food was delightful, and after dessert was served, Ray went to the podium to make some announcements. He thanked a variety of people and then shared with the 300-plus people in attendance that he was retiring in May, which elicited gasps from the audience. But the shock turned to anticipation as Ray announced that his replacements had just been solidified that morning and were here to share the new plans moving forward with all the honored and distinguished guests.

He then motioned for Max, who bounded to the podium, wasting no time introducing himself as the CEO of Cast the Net. As Max delineated the new vision for the mission and its partnership with JW Enterprises, the crowd broke into wild applause, rising to its collective feet in a standing ovation. While the crowd was enthusiastic, Max asked for a special round of applause and appreciation for Ray and Sally's 35 years of leading the mission. Phoebe brought the memory board in their honor to the stage, which provoked a second standing ovation, this one lasting for five minutes. Once everybody settled back down, Max introduced Jonah, Martha, and Abigail (although he decided not to put Missy on the spot before all of those people). Jonah talked off the cuff for five minutes, mesmerizing the room with his enthusiasm and entrepreneurial spirit. Martha then shared a quick vision for the Aunt Sally's shelters, and finally Abigail gave everyone instructions for the dance in the gym and the details of the silent auction's final totals. Heart and Soul had raised $45,000 through the silent auction. That would help pay off a couple of immediate bills with high interest rates, she told the enthusiastic crowd, sparing unnecessary details. She also thanked Big Beef and Big Jim himself, who yelled out that he was doubling down on his investment and would call Jonah in the morning. Finally, Abigail said, it was time for the Sweet Heart Dance, so she introduced one of Chicago's finest up-and-coming country bands, The Marauders.

The Marauders started with a slow and steady pace, to allow the participants to digest their food and get settled into their evening, before they turned up the volume and intensity, encouraging those who had been waiting for a sufficiently upbeat soundtrack for their dancing. About an hour in, Matt called Max up on stage to play a few songs with them. The crowd encouraged Max by chanting his name until he felt obliged to comply. The new CEO of the mission couldn't hide any parts of himself any longer. They played a couple of cover songs before launching into a couple of their original tunes. Max was having a blast. After the fifth song, Max asked Matt for the microphone and asked the band to cue up "Forever Love." Max asked the crowd if he could share the love story of Max and Abigail. After the crowd shouted out its approval, Max gave a three-minute history of their relationship, culminating in this public profession of his love tonight and the song they were about to play.

Abigail was embarrassed Max singled her out and made her stand in the middle of the dance floor with her family, but she was very honored at Max's public proclamation of their song. Then Max became more vulnerable, releasing 17 years of reserved and contained sentiment for the only woman he had ever loved. He had written it out while on the plane ride back to Florida, committing it to memory: "Abigail, I have loved you since the first time I saw you when we were ten years old. You are the only woman I have ever loved. You are the only woman I will ever love. You are kind. You are gentle. You are smart. You are compassionate. You are wise. When I am away from you, a part of me is missing: my heart. I apologize for the times I have not treated your heart with the same love, care, and respect I should have. I have not always cherished you, but that won't happen anymore. I have not always put our relationship ahead of my work, my ambition, and my toys, but *that* won't happen anymore. It is about time that I treat our relationship, and you, as the greatest gift God has given me. I love you forever, and forever is our love." He ended with the last line of the song, and – on cue – the band turned the volume back up as the crowd erupted into applause.

When the song was over, Matt told Max he was fired from the band, again, and needed to move to the dance floor with his future bride. Max and Abigail were in their own world. Abigail didn't care or even notice everyone was watching them, and Max was focused on only her. After the first chorus of "Endless Love," Matt invited everybody back onto the dance floor to join them. Martha and Jonah were the first couple to arrive, but when Jonah asked to cut in and switch partners, Max said no. They all laughed and agreed that was probably a wise decision. Max spun Abigail around several times, ending the dance with a dip and a kiss. Max then asked Abigail if he could talk to her outside for a minute, and the couple slowly worked their way through the crowd and out to the beach front. The last people they saw on their way out were Reginald and Felipe, huge smiles on their faces, who each gave Abigail a kiss and Max a high five.

The happy couple walked toward the beach and now looked every bit as much in love as Jonah and Martha had on that same path earlier in the day. Abigail thanked Max for the public declaration of love, though he didn't have to do that. She knew that he loved her. Max disagreed with her and told her he had to be true to who he was and allow authenticity to be aligned between his heart, soul, and mind. Far too often, he had allowed his mind to block his heart and soul. Too often, he had been too worried about bottom lines, about what other people thought, about his future, about his money, his looks, or his reputation. He was done with all of that forever. Abigail, moved by Max's passion for a new life, was inspired to do the same, so as she declared her love to him, she also admitted how scared and hurt she had been when Max hadn't seem totally invested in getting married. She stopped walking for a minute and faced Max.

She reiterated she had forgiven him, she had loved him for all 17 of those years, and she would marry him wherever and whenever he was ready. Max responded with a huge hug and told her this was good news – because he wanted to get married tomorrow, before he had to return to France. Abigail screamed with a resounding "YES!"

They made their way back to the celebration dance and enjoyed dancing and hanging out with all their family. Jonah and Martha were working the crowd as if Cast the Net were already well established, and with those two and Max and Abigail involved, it probably was. Ray and Sally looked totally relaxed, relieved, and exhausted . . . but joyful. What a night! The burden – the weight to keep the mission open – was finally off their hearts. Even more rewarding, their legacy would be carried out by their own family and their names would be honored and used to continue to serve the community they had loved for so long. Sally had already picked their first vacation. She wanted to go on an Alaskan cruise – somewhere that wasn't hot, where she wouldn't have to cook, somewhere beautiful and much different than Florida. Now that the new plan had been put into place, Ray and Sally decided to book the trip soon

and to leave in late May or June.

Chapter 22

Sunday

By 12:30 a.m., the Marauders were exhausted, but they had been a huge success. Missy, Phoebe, Mark, and Maisy had taken turns at the band's display table, and they had sold out of their CD's. They had also booked three more gigs in Florida. Missy had put a high surcharge on the fact that the band would have to travel. If the band let her, she would create a tour in the South that would be extremely profitable for all of them. After their last song, Max went to the stage to give the closing remarks, thanking everybody for their gifts of time, energy, and money. Max invited Phoebe up on stage so she could give a last tribute to Ray and Sally, which prompted another standing ovation. Taking the microphone back from Phoebe, Max said he had one more special announcement, but first he had to ask Jerry and Joan Richards a couple of questions. They obliged him and wandered sheepishly to the dance floor and by Abigail. First, Max asked, would Jerry and Joan give him permission to marry their daughter? They both gave a loud "yes," and the crowd cheered.

Max shared with the crowd that Jerry was an ordained minister in Illinois before asking his second question: Would Jerry be willing to marry them? Following an emphatic "yes," the crowd let out a bunch of whoops and hollers of appreciation. Lastly, Max asked if Jerry would marry them tomorrow at the beach at 11 a.m.? This time, before Jerry could even answer, the crowd went crazy. Max finally shushed the crowd so he could hear Jerry yell, "Absolutely! I'd love to." Max invited anyone and everyone to the wedding before wishing all a good night. There would never be another Valentine's Dance like this one.

The clean-up took a couple of hours, but Max and Abigail were not there, their families having sent them home to get some sleep before their big day. They also sent Ray and Sally home, so they wouldn't have to clean up after their last big celebration. There was more than enough help to allow the almost-newlyweds to get to bed. Besides, Max had to fly to France at 4:00 p.m. and deal with jet lag all over again. The rest of the family finally trudged back to their rooms by about 2:30 a.m., but nobody whined. They were too excited for the next day's wedding. Finally, by 3:00 a.m. the house fell silent. It had been a whirlwind of a week, but the capstone event was not the Valentine's Day Celebration, despite its enormous success. The culmination of the crazy Valentine's Day week would be the marriage of Max McGovern and Abigail Richards on the beach. There were also the budding relationships between Jonah Smith and Martha Kingsbury and between Matt McGovern and Missy Richards. It had been a wonderful week of drama, romance, and love.

Fatigue did not stop Sally from cooking a grand wedding-day breakfast, especially after she coerced Missy and Martha to help her – telling them it was about time they worked on their culinary skills since they were moving into a new stage of relationship with their men and with the shelter. Call Sally old-fashioned or stuck in her era, but the girls did not deny they needed to learn more in the kitchen. Everyone was called to breakfast by 9, and there was decent energy in the room, considering everyone's significant shortage of needed sleep. At about 9:15, Jerry and Joan arrived with the *Space Coast Daily* newspaper, which had wonderful write-ups about the celebration, the auction, the dance, the retirement, and the new leaders and vision. There was even an open invitation to the wedding. Joan also had brought a big box with her, and she excitedly placed it in front of Abigail and told her to open it. Abigail blushed and opened the box's lid. Inside was a white wedding dress. It was Abigail's wedding dress. Max had asked Joan to bring the dress with them from Chicago, just in case. Everyone laughed and applauded. Abigail wiped her tears away and asked her mom how she had finally believed it might be true after all the previous false starts. Joan told her it was because this time, Max was the one who was planning the potential wedding, and Max was the one taking the initiative.

The family went down to the beach at 10:45 a.m. Ray had received permission to host the marriage on the beach from some of the civil leaders that morning. He had to call in a few favors. The men had carried 100 chairs from the mission to the beach, and the ladies had done some quick decorations to at least give the moment some wedding ambiance. Matt and Mike brought their guitars down for some music, surprising Max and Abigail with an original song they had written for the marriage – five years ago. They had rehearsed it a couple of times a year, just in case. It was good to finally get to perform it. Max had Ray, Jonah, Mike, Matt, Reginald, and Felipe stand with him; Abigail had Sally, Missy, Phoebe, Stephanie, Martha and her mom. Only the wedding couple was in formal attire, with everyone else in their casual beach clothes. By the time the service was ready to start, there were well over 200 people there.

The processional guitar music started, and everyone rose as Abigail walked down the makeshift sand aisle. Pastor Jerry started off the service with a welcome and a prayer, after which Reginald and Felipe read their favorite Scripture verses about love. Matt and Mike then played their new song – "I Always Knew" – with a chorus that said, "I always knew it was you. I always knew it was you. From the first time I saw you and every day after, I always knew it was you." The crowd whistled and cheered for the next Marauders single while the brothers joined Max in the wedding party. Pastor Jerry then led the couple in their vows, the exchange of rings, and, fittingly for the setting, the unity sand ritual. The couple chose red, black, and silver as their colors of unity based on their high school colors and the colors they had used for the Cast the Net website ten years prior, when they had first dreamt of its now-impending existence.

Phoebe sang "Amazing Grace" after the unity sand, inviting everyone to join in for the last verse and chorus. Finally, Pastor Jerry pronounced his daughter and son-in law to be officially married and invited Max to kiss his bride – which he did, to more cheers. The happy couple walked back down the sand aisle, took a sharp right turn, and ran into the ocean. The bridal party followed. Soon, there were at least a hundred people frolicking in the water.

Sally, Joan, and Maisy had prepared some light lunch fare, but as soon as Jonah saw the size of the crowd, he slipped his credit card to one of the young men watching, asking him to go grab another $300 worth of food at the nearby convenience store. The kid took a few friends with him, and Jonah told them they could each buy themselves a little something as well. He needed the food back to the kitchen as soon as possible, and if they didn't leave his credit card in the refrigerator, he would have the FBI on the beach within an hour. Most everybody except the tourists stayed to talk, eat, swim, and enjoy the Marauders playing an unplugged set on the veranda – after they had changed into some dry clothes. The wedding really couldn't have gone much better even with more than 12 hours advanced planning. Max and Abigail were so glad they had done it this way. It beat the hassles and the burden of planning a wedding while an ocean apart, and they hadn't had to worry about tons of expectations from either side of the family, with hundreds of minor and insignificant details. There was no time. They would still hold a reception in Chicago when Max came back from Paris so that their Chicago friends and community could celebrate with them. Besides, Stephanie wanted to make sure that Max would invite Renaldo so she could see him again.

Abigail had one more major responsibility for the day. She had to call Mary Anne, the second week in a row with difficult news. She told Mary Anne she was putting in her two-week notice, she had just married Max on the beach, and they were both moving to Florida to take over the mission. Mary Anne was very happy for Abigail but would not allow Abigail to work with her for two weeks. She told her that she was fired, but with a nice severance package, including a ticket to fly to Paris as a honeymoon gift. Abigail couldn't believe the blessing and screamed at Max as soon as she got off the phone that she was going to Paris with him. They both hugged and celebrated until they remembered they had only 45 minutes to change, pack, and leave for the airport. What an absolute whirlwind the last three days had been. What a joy and blessing it was to finally be married. They ran into the house and saw Ray and Sally sipping some wine on the veranda, watching their extended family play and celebrate on the beach and in their house. Ten days ago, they had thought their rescue mission was about ready to close. Now it had been purchased by a philanthropist who allowed Ray to stay in a capacity of leadership and who named the women's shelters – all of them – after Sally. Max and Abigail stopped for a moment on their way through the veranda to the house. Max and Ray looked at the couple, huge smiles on their faces, and said in one voice, "It's about time."

About the Author

Elliott J. Anderson is a Pastor, Professor, Counselor, Contractor, Drummer, Author, and an eternal romantic. He is married to Angie and father of Eliah, Jacob, Alivia, Paige, and their dog Twinkie. Elliott and Angie are also licensed foster parents. Elliott's previous books are Simon Says, Principles and Perspectives from Dr. Simon V. Anderson, Clifton Hills Press 2020, and Answers in Abundance, A Miraculous Adoption Journey As Told From A Father's Heart, Morgan James Publishing 2007.

Made in the USA
Monee, IL
28 February 2021

61565022R00128